不朽奇幻童話經典

愛麗絲夢遊仙境

Alice's Adventures in Wonderland

中英雙語版

路易斯 · 凱洛———著

曾銘祥———繪

李漢昭———譯

晨星出版

愛藏本087

愛麗絲夢遊仙境【中英雙語版】
Alice's Adventures in Wonderland

作　　者｜路易斯‧凱洛（Lewis Carroll）
繪　　者｜約翰‧田尼爾（John Tenniel）、曾銘祥
譯　　者｜李漢昭

責任編輯｜林儀涵
封面設計｜黃斐文
美術編輯｜黃偵瑜

創 辦 人｜陳銘民
發 行 所｜晨星出版有限公司
　　　　　台中市407工業區30路1號
　　　　　TEL：04-23595820　FAX：04-23550581
　　　　　E-mail: service@morningstar.com.tw
　　　　　http://www.morningstar.com.tw
　　　　　行政院新聞局局版台業字第2500號

總 經 銷｜知己圖書股份有限公司
　　　　　台北市106辛亥路一段30號9樓
　　　　　TEL：02-23672044 / 23672047　FAX：02-23635741
　　　　　台中市407工業區30路1號1樓
　　　　　TEL：04-23595819　FAX：04-23595493
　　　　　E-mail：service@morningstar.com.tw
　　　　　網路書店 http://www.morningstar.com.tw
法律顧問｜陳思成律師
郵政劃撥｜15060393（知己圖書股份有限公司）
服務專線｜04-23595819#230

印　　刷｜上好印刷股份有限公司

出版日期｜2016年04月15日二版1刷
再版日期｜2021年05月30日二版2刷
定　　價｜新台幣250元
ISBN 978-986-443-116-8
Printed in Taiwan
All Right Reserved
版權所有‧翻印必究
如有缺頁或破損，請寄回更換

國家圖書館出版品預行編目資料
愛麗絲夢遊仙境／路易斯‧凱洛（Lewis Carroll）著；李漢昭譯
臺中市：晨星，2016.04
愛藏本；87
譯自：Alice's Adventures in Wonderland
ISBN 978-986-443-116-8（平裝）
CIP 873.59　105002129

找尋自己的愛麗絲

ALICE'S ADVENTURES IN WONDERLAND

作家／甘耀明

相信很多人在讀過完整版《愛麗絲夢遊仙境》之前，已透過繪本、漫畫或卡通等方式，捷足瞭解了小說中的經典情節，例如：愛麗絲忽而膨脹、忽而縮小的情節；再者如撲克牌紅心國王所召開的那場像「扮家家酒」的審判庭等，皆說明了這本小說已經成了大家童年經驗的一部分。

我讀小學時，經由卡通版第一次進入愛麗絲的夢境，深深的被愛麗絲與撲克牌紅心皇后打槌球的場面吸引。在那場槌球遊戲之前，愛麗絲因為沒有跪下恭迎紅心皇后的龐大隊伍，惹得脾氣暴躁的紅心皇后下令砍她的頭。接下來的槌球遊戲中，簡直滑稽無比，刺蝟成了槌球，紅鶴成了槌球棒，演出一場動

003

物嘉年華會。愛麗絲用槌棒打球時，紅鶴的脖子老是會伸縮轉彎，等到她會控制紅鶴的脾氣時，慢吞吞的刺蝟早就不耐煩的走了，直到愛麗絲說服刺蝟要守本分後，弓起腰作為球門的撲克牌士兵竟跑去散步了。槌球場最後又成了一場混仗，無怪紅心皇后又暴跳如雷的大喊：「砍掉你們的頭！」

那時候，我滿心期待紅心皇后的「暴力語言」成真，能砍下誰的頭顱，但是一直到愛麗絲夢醒前，沒有任何角色的頭被砍下來。我期待的並不是誰的頭被砍下後的死亡場面，而是被砍頭的角色會如何更顯明的活下去。那顆頭會被當成槌球？然後大喊：「你們不會打輕一點嗎？」或者成為小說中消失身體的柴郡貓，整個頭顱浮在空中耍寶？我之所以會這樣想，是因為了解《愛麗絲夢遊仙境》的風格不是處理死亡，而是在展現逗趣幽默的世界。如今看來，這本小說讓童年時的我創造一個岔出的情節，是閱讀中再創造的樂趣，無形中也創造出自己的一個「愛麗絲幻境」。

《愛麗絲夢遊仙境》是作者路易斯·凱洛（Lewis Carroll，1832~1898）

的第一本小說。他是英國牛津大學的數學教師，生性害羞，且有口吃，但喜歡與小孩子相處，在語言、插畫及攝影等方面都有傑出表現。他是家中長子，父親是幽默感十足的牧師，或許是這些因素，提供《愛麗絲夢遊仙境》中角色的擬人化、孩童性格及風趣對話。《愛麗絲夢遊仙境》的小說雛形，是路易斯·凱洛對該學院主任的三個女兒所講的故事，經過整理及修潤後，以童話的形式風靡全世界。

細心的讀者或許會發現，故事中有不少括弧說明，例如多多鳥說：「要說明它嗎？最好的方法就是我們親自做做看。」（如果你也想在冬天玩這種遊戲，我可以在這裡告訴你多多鳥是怎麼做的。）

這其實是留下「說故事」過程中，成人與小孩的互動痕跡。路易斯·凱洛用豐沛的想像力說故事時，小女孩可能會不斷問：「為什麼？」、「然後呢？」此時他難免要解釋一番；或者他在觀察小女孩聽故事的表情反應時，適切加入自己的說明。一旦小女孩漸漸著迷於路易斯·凱洛所說的故事後，也就

是進行到故事後半段了，那些括弧說明也淡出了故事，由情節的推演掌控了一切。

《愛麗絲夢遊仙境》是一本好看、有趣的小說，適合大人小孩閱讀，甚至作為「奇幻小說」入門是再適合不過了。但是，一位大人在閱畢這本小說後，若是只能讚嘆說出：「這是一本好看、有趣的小說。」則顯然忽略了小說中所傳達的更深刻意涵。

《愛麗絲夢遊仙境》以無厘頭、幽默諷刺、語言遊戲、口白描述的方式描寫小孩眼中的世界，相信不少人讀完這本小說後，會發出會心微笑，甚至捧腹大笑。但是，在笑聲背後，讀者會發現這樣迷魅的夢境，顯然已經在大人生活中逐漸消失。我可以在《愛麗絲夢遊仙境》中隨意找出例子，當獅鷲向愛麗絲說起鱈魚的故事，出現了以下對話：

「海裡的靴子和鞋子，」獅鷲嗓音深沉地繼續說：「是用鱈魚的雪擦的。

「現在你知道了。」

「那鱈魚的雪是用什麼做的？」愛麗絲好奇地追問。

「當然是鯧魚和鰻魚啦！」獅鷲顯得很不耐煩，「就算是小蝦子也會這樣告訴你的。」

套句新世代人類的口語來說，這些對話真像「地球人」與「外星人」之間的對談。用大人的眼光來看，這些話不是「事實」，再爭辯下去會使「生活效率」打折，經濟效益蒙受損失。但是，我認為這段話的意義不在於「鱈魚的雪」是不是能當成鞋油來擦靴子，而是展現小孩子如何透過摸索，創造自己的世界，在不斷尋找的過程中，一位內心充滿「為什麼」的小孩也許找到全新的世界，也許不是，但是大膽實驗的過程就是一種成長。這種能力，反而在大人身上逐漸消失，他們習慣吃同一種食物、走同一條路回家、看同樣的電視節目，然後做同一種夢想，直到幻滅為止。

在我看來，《愛麗絲夢遊仙境》最有趣的地方是在荒謬情節背後所展現的意義。在〈瘋狂茶會〉中，三月兔、帽匠及睡鼠的時間一直停在下午茶時段，

彼此在對談上大玩語言遊戲，每隔一段起身換座位，他們的手錶只是用來報日期，並非報時間，而且「只要你喜歡，時間都可以撥到哪」。如果時間是可以任意調整的工具，那麼角色當然可以拒絕成長，永遠活在相同的記憶中，生活變得毫無生趣，連愛麗絲都大嘆：「這是我這輩子見過最愚蠢的茶會了。」

〈假海龜的故事〉這段情節裡，孤獨又悲傷的假海龜，眼珠老是泡在自己的淚水裡，一開始便說：「我曾經是隻真正的海龜。」但是從頭到尾，這隻偽裝悲傷的假海龜只談論自己光榮的過往，甚至大唱「海龜湯」便宜又好喝，卻始終沒有瞭解自己為何會變「假」，察明那個「真」的自己為何會變質。

到了小說最後的法庭審判段落，更彰顯情節的荒謬，為了定讞紅心傑克偷水果塔的罪行，整個法庭像市場般鬧哄哄的上演。十二位審判員在記事板上寫下自己名字──「笨東西」，以免審判後自己忘祖忘宗；證人之一的帽匠出席時，反而被狡猾的法官扣上「小偷」這大帽子，無言以對；另一位證人女廚師才出席作證，馬上在慌亂中落跑了；至於什麼都不曉得的愛麗絲，也被傳喚為

證人，因出言反駁庭上，竟激怒了皇后，下令要砍愛麗絲。這場砸派似的鬧劇，是在愛麗絲的夢醒後結束，當然，夢醒之後，讀者很難忘記愛麗絲是如何天真爛漫地帶領大家，出入一個成人早已遺忘的夢鄉。

順帶一提的是，如果讀者看完這本小說，可以準備一本筆記本，紀錄自己的睡夢情節。你將會發現，夢中世界是多麼吻合《愛麗絲夢遊仙境》的情境，再整理這本夢的筆記簿，屬於自己的《愛麗絲夢遊仙境》就誕生了。如果你真誠地看待自己的夢，或許有那麼一天，你會發現屬於自己的愛麗絲，已經躲在夢的角落太久了，等待你的擁抱。

愛麗絲夢遊仙境・目錄

ALICE'S ADVENTURES IN WONDERLAND

第一章　掉進兔子洞

愛麗絲坐在河岸邊，無所事事地靠在姐姐身上，她偷偷瞄了一眼姐姐正在看的書，書裡沒有圖畫，也沒有對話。愛麗絲心想：「沒有圖畫，也沒有對話的書，有什麼意思呢？」

悶熱的天氣讓愛麗絲昏昏欲睡，她心想，是否該起身採些雛菊做個花環呢？此時，一隻粉紅色眼睛的白兔突然跑過她身邊。

一隻粉紅色眼睛的兔子經過身邊，不是什麼值得大驚小怪的事，甚至於聽到兔子自言自語說著：「喔天哪！喔天哪！我要遲到了！」愛麗絲也沒有覺得很離奇。（雖然事後回想起來，她覺得她應該要很驚訝的，可是當時一切好像都很自然。）

此時，兔子突然停下腳步，從背心口袋中掏出一隻懷錶，看一看之後又匆匆跑走。愛麗絲這才跳起來，腦中閃過一個念頭：從來沒見過穿著背心的兔子，甚至還掏出懷錶來！她壓抑不住自己的好奇心，緊跟著兔子穿過田野，看見兔子鑽進灌木叢下的大洞。愛麗絲不顧一切跟著跳進去，根本沒有考慮之後是否出得來。

兔子洞一開始像條走廊，筆直地向前延伸，後來就突然直通向下。愛麗絲還來不及止步，就往一個深井般的通道直直墜落。

也許是通道太長太深，也許是下落的速度太慢，愛麗絲往下掉的同時還有時間一邊東張西望，一邊猜測接下來會發生什麼事。一開始，她努力往下看，想知道最後會掉到什麼地方，但是底下一片漆黑，什麼也看不見。於是她轉而看向四周的井壁，井壁上排滿了碗櫥和書架，以及掛在釘子上的地圖和圖畫。她順手從架子上拿了一個罐頭，上面寫著「橘子果醬」，令她大失所望的是，罐子裡面是空的。

她不敢把空罐頭扔掉，怕砸到下面的人。因

此，當她繼續往下掉的時候，她想辦法把空罐頭放到另一個碗櫥裡去。

「好吧！」愛麗絲心想，「我摔過了這麼一大跤，以後要是我再從樓梯上滾下來，那也沒什麼大不了的！家裡的人一定都會誇獎我真是勇敢，為什麼，因為即便以後我再從屋頂上掉下來，我也一句話都不會說的！」（這點倒很可能是真的。）

掉啊，掉啊，掉啊，這一跤永遠都跌不到底部嗎？「我不知道掉了多少公里？」愛麗絲大聲說著：「我一定已經靠近地球中心的某個地方了。讓我算算看⋯⋯已經墜落大約六千公里了，一定有⋯⋯」（看吧，愛麗絲在學校已經學到一點東西，儘管現在不是展現知識的好時機，因為根本沒人聽她說話，不過練習說說也好。）「⋯⋯沒錯，大概就是這個距離──但是，不知道在什麼經緯度呢？」（愛麗絲既不明白什麼是經度，也不明白什麼是緯度，只是認為這個字眼很棒，聽起來還蠻有深度的。）

過一會兒後，她又說話：「不知道我會不會穿過地球？如果我一出去就能

遇見那些頭朝下走路的人，那該多有趣啊！這叫做反感世界吧？」這次她很高興沒有人聽見她說話，因為她自己也覺得她用錯詞了。「不過，我想我得問問他們的國家叫什麼名字。夫人，請問這裡是紐西蘭還是澳洲呢？」（她一邊說一邊試著行屈膝禮──從空中往下掉時還行屈膝禮！你覺得你有辦法想像這個畫面？）「可是如果我真的這樣問，他們一定會把我當成傻孩子，連自己在什麼國家都不知道。」愛麗絲心裡又想：「不，絕對不能這麼問，也許我會在某個地方看到國名的標示吧！」

掉啊，掉啊，掉啊，除此之外沒有別的事可做，於是愛麗絲又開始講起話來：「我敢說黛娜今晚一定會想我。（黛娜是她的貓。）希望他們沒有忘記下午茶時間給她一碟牛奶。我的乖黛娜，真希望你現在跟我一起往下掉。可是恐怕空中沒有你要吃的老鼠，不過或許你可以抓到一隻蝙蝠，蝙蝠很像老鼠，你知道的。可是貓吃不吃蝙蝠呢？」

愛麗絲有些睏了，但依舊迷迷糊糊地自言自語：「貓吃蝙蝠嗎？貓吃蝙蝠

嗎？」然後有的時候是：「蝙蝠吃貓嗎？」不過這兩個問題她都答不出來，所以不管怎麼樣問都無所謂。她睡著了，開始做夢來。她夢見自己和黛娜正手拉著手散步，並且認真地問：「黛娜，跟我說實話，你到底有沒有吃過蝙蝠？」突然間，砰！砰！她掉到一堆乾枯的枝葉上，總算不再往下掉了。

愛麗絲沒有摔傷，她馬上跳起來，向上一看，頭頂一片漆黑。往前一看，又是一條長長的

通道，她看見那隻白兔正急急忙忙地往前跑。這回可別跟丟了，愛麗絲像一陣風似地馬上追過去。她聽見兔子在轉彎時說著：「哎呀，我的耳朵和鬍子，都這麼晚了！」當時她仍然緊跟在後，可是一過轉角，兔子就不見了。她發現自己來到一個長長的、低矮的走廊，屋頂上掛著一長排的燈，將走廊照得通亮。

走廊四周全是門，但都上了鎖。愛麗絲從頭走到尾，推一推、拉一拉，沒有一扇門打得開，她愁眉苦臉地來到走廊中央，思索她該怎麼出去。

突然間，她發現一張玻璃三腳桌。桌上除了一把小小的金鑰匙，什麼也沒有。愛麗絲立刻想到這把鑰匙可能是用來開啓其中一扇門的。可是，哎呀，不是鎖孔太大，就是鑰匙太小，她試了一輪，打不開任何一扇門。不過，在繞第

二圈時，她發現一個先前沒注意到的矮簾子，簾子後面有一扇約四十八公分高的小門。她把小金鑰匙插進門鎖裡，太好了，剛剛好。

愛麗絲打開門，看見一條小通道，不比老鼠洞大，她跪下來，順著通道望出去，看到一個非常可愛的小花園。她多想從這個黑暗的長廊走出去，到美麗的花園和清涼噴泉中玩耍！可是那門小的連頭都過不去，可憐的愛麗絲心想：

「哎，就算頭能過得去，肩膀過不去也沒用，真希望自己能縮小，像望遠鏡裡看到的那樣！我想我一定有辦法變小的，只要我知道該怎麼做。」你看，發生了這麼多稀奇古怪的事，愛麗絲認為世界上幾乎什麼事都是有可能的。

一直守在小門旁空等也不是辦法，於是愛麗絲又回到桌子旁，希望再找到一把鑰匙，或者找到一本教人如何縮小的書。這次，她在桌上發現一個小瓶子，（愛麗絲說：「它剛才絕對不在這裡。」）瓶口上繫著一張小紙條，上面寫著兩個很漂亮的大字⋯⋯「喝我」。

「喝我」這個建議很不錯，可是聰明的小愛麗絲並不打算立刻匆匆忙忙地照

做。「不行，我要先檢查一下，」她說，「看看瓶子上面有沒有寫著『毒藥』這個字眼。」因為她聽過一些很不錯的故事，關於小孩子被燒傷、被野獸吃掉，以及其他一些可怕的事情，全都是因為他們沒有把大人說過的話放在心上，例如：火鉗握得太久就會把手燒壞；用小刀割手指就會出血；還有一點，她也牢記在心：如果把寫著「毒藥」瓶裡的藥水喝進肚子，肯定會完蛋。

然而，這個瓶子上並沒有寫著「毒藥」的字樣，於是愛麗絲大膽地嚐了一口，味道很好，混合著櫻桃水果塔、奶油蛋糕、鳳梨、烤火雞、牛奶糖、熱奶油麵包的味道。愛麗絲一口氣就把一整瓶喝光了。

「好奇怪的感覺喔！」愛麗絲說：「我一定是像望遠鏡裡那樣變小了。」

果然，現在的她只有二十五公分高了，大小正好可以穿過小門到那個可愛的花園去。她高興得眉飛色舞。不過，她又等了幾分鐘，看看自己會不會繼續縮小下去。想到這點，她開始有點緊張了。「結果會怎麼樣呢？」愛麗絲對自己說，「也許我會一直縮小下去，就像蠟燭的火苗那樣到最後全部熄滅。那我

會怎麼樣呢？」於是她又努力想像蠟燭熄滅後的火焰。可是想了半天也想不出來，因為她不記得自己曾經見過那樣的東西。

過了一會兒，好像沒有再發生什麼事，她決定立刻到花園去。但是，唉呀！可憐的愛麗絲！她走到小門前，才發覺自己忘了拿那把小金鑰匙。等她走回桌子旁，卻發現自己太矮了，根本拿不到鑰匙。

透過透明的玻璃桌面她可以清楚地看到鑰匙，她盡力攀著桌腳向上爬，可是實在是太滑了。可憐的小愛麗絲一次又一次地從桌腳溜下來，累得精疲力竭，於是她坐在地上開始嚎啕大哭。

「起來！像你哭成這樣是沒用的！」愛麗絲語氣嚴厲地對自己說：「我建議你最好在一分鐘內停止哭泣！」她常常給自己一些很不錯的建議（話雖如此，但她很少照做），然後有時候罵自己罵得太兇，還把自己罵哭了；還有一次她在和自己比賽槌球時作了弊，結果打了自己一巴掌。這個古怪的孩子很喜歡假裝同時扮成兩個人。「可是現在沒有用了，」可憐的小愛麗絲想，「假裝

自己是兩個人！為什麼，因為現在我小到沒辦法當一個完整的人了！」

不久，愛麗絲看見桌子底下有一個小玻璃盒。她打開一看，裡面有塊很小的蛋糕，用葡萄乾寫著「吃我」。「好，我就吃它，」愛麗絲說：「如果它能使我變大，我就能拿得到那把鑰匙了；如果它使我變得更小，那我就可以從門縫下面爬過去。反正只要能讓我到那個花園去，不管怎麼變都可以。」

她咬了一小口，就焦急地自言自語：「是哪一種？變大還是變小？」她把手放在頭頂，摸摸看往上還是往下，卻驚訝地發現一點也沒變。吃蛋糕本來是很正常的事，可是愛麗絲太期待會發生一些稀奇古怪的事，因此這些很正常的事反倒顯得枯燥乏味了。於是，她開始大口吃起來，很快就把一塊蛋糕吃完。

如果你遇見一隻拿著懷錶的奇妙兔子，會不會也像愛麗絲一樣跟著牠跳進兔子洞裡去？

第二章　眼淚池

「奇怪，這真是太奇怪了！」愛麗絲驚訝到頓時啞口無言，「現在我一定大得像世界上最大的望遠鏡了。再見了，我的腿呀！」（她低頭一看，腳快遠得看不見了。）「喔，我可憐的小腳啊！不知道以後誰幫你們穿襪子和繫鞋帶呢？肯定不會是我了，我離你們太遠太了，沒辦法再照顧你們，以後你們只好自己照顧自己！……不過，我一定會好好對待它們的，不然它們會不願走到我想去的地方。對，每年聖誕節的時後我一定要送它們一雙新靴子。」

她繼續想著該怎樣送：「一定要交給送貨的人送過去，真好笑，寄禮物給自己的腳！收件地址寫起來不是更好笑嗎？

愛麗絲的右腳收

壁爐前的地毯

愛你的愛麗絲寄

就在這一剎那，她的
頭撞到大廳的屋頂。現在
她至少有二百多公分高，
她急忙拿起小金鑰匙，向
小花園門前跑去。

「噢，天哪，我在胡說
八道些什麼呀！」

可憐的愛麗絲！她只能側身躺在地上，用一隻眼睛往花園裡看，想進去根
本就不可能，於是坐在地上又哭了起來。

「你不覺得難爲情嗎？」愛麗絲對自己說，「像你這麼大的女孩（說得很對），還這樣哭個不停。馬上給我停下來！立刻停下來！」但她還是不停地哭，一滴眼淚可以裝滿一個水桶，一桶一桶的眼淚流個不停，直到身邊變成一個大水池，足足有十公分深，把半個大廳都淹沒。

過一會兒，她聽見遠處傳來輕微的腳步聲，急忙擦乾眼淚，原來那隻小白兔又回來了，打扮得十分講究，一隻手拿著一雙白色羊皮手套，另一隻手握著一把大扇子，正急急忙忙地跑過來。牠邊跑邊喃喃自語：「哎呀，公爵夫人！要是讓她久等，該不會就要大發雷霆了吧！」愛麗絲非常希望有人可以來幫她一下，雖然她很不喜歡開口請別人幫她，但當小白兔一走近，她還是低聲說：

「不好意思，先生……」兔子嚇一大跳，連白色羊皮手套和扇子都扔到一旁，拼命朝暗處跑去。

愛麗絲把扇子和手套撿起來。屋裡很熱，她一邊搧著扇子，一邊自言自語：「天啊！今天可全是些怪事，昨天一切都還那麼正常，不知道是不是晚上

發生了什麼事？讓我想想……我早上起來時是不是還是我自己？我想起來了，早上就覺得有點不對勁。但是，如果我不是自己的話，那我又是誰呢？啊！這可真是個謎啊！」接著她把自己認識的同齡孩子都想過一遍，看看自己是不是變成她們其中一個。

「肯定不是愛達，」愛麗絲說：「因為她有長長的捲髮，而我的頭髮一點都不捲；肯定也不是瑪貝爾，因為我懂得許許多多的事情，而她，哼！她什麼都不知道。再說，她是她，我是我，喔！天哪！越想越糊塗了，真傷腦筋啊！讓我來試試看，看我還記不記得過去知道的事情。讓我想想……四乘五是十二，四乘六是十三，四乘七是……唉，這樣下去一輩子都到不了二十；況且九九乘法表本來就沒什麼意思。再來試試地理好了……倫敦是巴黎的首都，而巴黎是羅馬的首都，羅馬是……不，不，全錯了。我一定……一定是變成瑪貝爾了。讓我再來試試背《……小鱷魚》──」她像朗誦課文一樣，雙手交叉放在膝蓋上，一本正經地背起來。她的聲音聽起來沙啞古怪，用字也和平時不一樣……

小鱷魚究竟怎麼做

使牠發亮的尾巴更閃亮，

把尼羅河水灑在身上

金光閃閃的鱗甲！

看牠笑得多麼快樂，

伸開爪子的姿勢多麼優雅，

歡迎那些小魚

游進牠溫柔微笑的嘴巴。

「我一定背錯了，」可憐的愛麗絲一邊說著，一邊淚眼汪汪的，「我一定是變成瑪貝爾了，這下子我得住在那間破房子裡，什麼玩具都沒有，哎，還得做那麼多功課。不！我拿定主意了，如果我變成了瑪貝爾，我就待在這井底，

就算他們把頭伸到井口說『上來吧！親愛的！』也沒有用。我只會抬頭問他們：『你們得先告訴我，我是誰，如果我變成我喜歡的人，我就上來，要不然，我就一直待在這裡，除非我再變成別人』⋯⋯」

「可是，天哪！」愛麗絲突然又哭了起來，「我真希望他們來叫我上去！一個人在這裡孤零零的好難受呀！」

她說話時，無意間看了一眼自己的手，大吃一驚，發現一隻手上戴了小白兔的白色羊皮手套。「怎麼會呢？」她想，「我一定又變小了。」她站起來走到桌子旁，量一量自己，正如她猜測的那樣，現在她大約只有五公分高了，而且還在迅速縮小中。她很快就發現是手上拿的那把扇子在作怪，於是連忙扔掉扇子，總算沒有縮得完全消失。

「好險！」愛麗絲真的嚇壞了，不過發現自己還好好的存在著，才放下心來。「現在可以去花園了！」她飛快跑到小門邊，可是，哎呀！小門又鎖上了，小金鑰匙像原來一樣仍然在玻璃桌上。「現在更糟了，」可憐的小愛麗絲

想，「我從來沒有這麼小過，從來沒有！這真是太糟了！真是太糟了！」

說著她腳底一滑，「撲通」一聲滑倒了，鹹鹹的池水淹到她的下巴。她的第一個念頭是她可能掉進海裡了「這樣一來，我就可以坐火車回去了！」她自言自語地說。（愛麗絲去過一次海邊，她以為每一個海灘上都有許多更衣車，有孩子在沙灘上用木鏟挖洞玩，有一棟棟的出租公寓，屋後總有一個火車站。）然而，她很快就明白，自己是在一個眼淚池裡，是她二百多公分高的時候哭出來的眼淚。

「唉！要是剛才沒哭得這麼厲害就好了！」愛麗絲邊說邊游，想找條路游出去，「我真是自作自受，被自己的眼淚淹死！這真是件怪事，不過說真的，今天一直碰到怪事！」此時，她聽到不遠處有划水聲，於是向前游去，想看個究竟。最初，她以為那一定是海象或河馬，後來她想起自己已經這麼小了，於是立刻明白，那不過是隻老鼠，像自己一樣不小心掉進水裡的。

「和一隻老鼠講話不知道有沒有用？」愛麗絲想，「這裡的事情都那麼不

尋常，也許牠會說話也不一定，無論如何，試一下也不會怎麼樣。」於是，愛麗絲說：「喂，老鼠！你認得出去的路嗎？我在這裡游得累死了。喂，老鼠！」愛麗絲認為和老鼠說話，一定要這樣稱呼才對。以前，她從沒這麼說過，不過她記得在哥哥的拉丁文語法書中看到：「主格，一隻老鼠——所有格，一隻老鼠的——與格，對一隻老鼠——稱呼格，喂，老鼠！」那隻老鼠狐疑地看著她，似乎還對她眨了眨眼睛，但沒有說話。

「也許牠不懂英語，」愛麗絲想，「牠一定是一隻法國老鼠，和威廉一世一起來的。」（儘管愛麗絲念過許多歷史知識，可是什麼事發生在什麼年代還是搞不清楚。）於是，她又用法語說：「我的貓咪在哪裡？」這是她的法文課本教的第一句話。

老鼠一聽到這句話，突然跳出水面，嚇得渾身發抖。愛麗絲怕傷害到這個可憐的小傢伙，趕緊說：「對不起！我都忘了你是不喜歡貓的。」

「我當然不喜歡貓啊！」老鼠尖聲地叫嚷：「要是你是我的話，你會喜歡

貓嗎？」

「嗯，可能不會吧，」愛麗絲柔聲地說：「你別生氣了。不過我還是希望你能看看我的貓咪黛娜，我想要是你見過她，就會喜歡貓了。她那麼可愛又那麼乖，」愛麗絲一面懶洋洋地游著，一面自言自語地繼續說：「她坐在火爐旁邊呼嚕呼嚕，還不時舔舔爪子，洗洗臉，摸起來軟綿綿的。還有，說到抓老鼠，她可是一流的……喔，對不起，對不起！」愛麗絲連忙道歉，因為這次真把老鼠氣壞了。愛麗絲說：「你要是不想聽，我們就不說她了。」

「還說『我們』呢！」老鼠從鬍子到尾巴都在發抖，「好像我願意聽你講這種事一樣！我們整個家族都最討厭貓了，那種噁心、下流、粗鄙的東西！不要再讓我聽到牠們的名字了！」

「好，好，我不會再提了啦，真的！」愛麗絲說著，急忙想轉換話題，「你……喜歡……喜歡……狗嗎？」老鼠沒有回答，於是愛麗絲熱切地說下去，「告訴你，我家隔壁有一隻可愛的小狗，一隻有著明亮眼睛的小獵狗，真

想帶牠來讓你看看。你知道嗎，牠全身長滿了長長的棕色捲毛。隨便你扔什麼東西，牠都會把它叼回來，還會坐下來討吃的，而且會玩好多好多的把戲。牠是一個農夫養的，知道嗎，那個農夫說牠很有用處，要價一百英鎊呢！還說牠能殺掉所有的田鼠，而且……哎呀，天哪！」愛麗絲後悔自己又說錯話了，「恐怕我又惹牠生氣了！」這回老鼠已經拼命游開了，還將池水攪動得翻騰不已。

愛麗絲跟在老鼠的後面好聲好氣地叫牠……「親愛的老鼠啊！你回來吧！如果你不喜歡，我們就再也不談貓呀狗呀的了！」老鼠聽到這話，轉過身慢慢地向她游近，牠的臉色蒼白（愛麗絲想牠一定是太生氣了），用低沉顫抖的聲音說：「我們上岸吧！我會告訴你我的過去，你就會明白我為什麼那麼討厭貓和狗了。」

是時候該走了，因為池塘裡已經擠滿了一大群鳥類和野獸……一隻鴨子、一隻多多鳥、一隻鸚鵡、一隻小鷹和一些稀奇古怪的動物。愛麗絲帶頭，和這群鳥獸一起向岸邊游去。

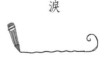

想一想

你也有過在水裡游泳的經驗嗎？都是在游泳池或是到海邊去？海水和眼淚嚐起來有什麼不一樣？

第三章 決策式競賽與一個很長的故事

聚集在岸上的一大群動物，樣子看起來稀奇古怪──羽毛濕漉漉的鳥、毛緊貼著身體的小動物，一個個渾身都濕淋淋的，又不高興又不好受地站著，顯得很狼狽。

現在第一個問題是，要怎樣把身體弄乾。他們商量了一會兒。過不了多久，愛麗絲很自然地和牠們混熟了，熟得好像老朋友似的。她和鸚鵡爭辯了好長的時間，惹得鸚鵡生氣了，不斷地說：「我歲數比你大，肯定比你知道得多。」愛麗絲不知道牠到底有多大，因此很不服氣，但是鸚鵡又拒絕說出牠的年齡，所以就無話可說了。

最後，那隻老鼠──牠在大家當中好像很有權威──高聲說道：「你們大

家都坐下，聽我說！我會很快把你們弄乾的！」他們都立即坐下，圍成一個大圈，老鼠坐在中間。愛麗絲也焦急不安地盯著牠，因為她知道如果不馬上把身體弄乾，一定會得重感冒。

「嗯！」老鼠煞有其事地哼了一聲，說：「你們都準備好了嗎？請大家全都安靜，這是我所知道的最乾巴巴的事情：威廉大將的事業得到教皇的支持，英國人很快就完全臣服於他，他們也需要有人領導，而且已經習慣於

被篡權和征服了。梅西亞和諾森勃列亞的伯爵埃德溫和莫卡……」

「啊！」鸚鵡又打了個冷顫。

「你怎麼了嗎！」老鼠皺了皺眉頭，但還是彬彬有禮地問道：「你有話要說嗎？」

「沒有，我沒有什麼要說的！」鸚鵡連忙回答道。

「我以為你有話要說呢！」老鼠說：「那我接著講下去，這兩個地方的伯爵埃德溫和莫卡都聲明支持威廉，甚至坎特伯雷非常愛國的大主教斯蒂坎德也發現這是明智的……」

「發現什麼？」鴨子問。

「發現『這』，」老鼠不耐煩地回答：「你應該知道『這』的意思。」

「我發現吃的東西時，當然知道『這』是指什麼，『這』通常指一隻青蛙或一條蚯蚓。但現在的問題是，大主教發現了什麼？」鴨子呱啦叫著。

老鼠完全不理會牠的問題，忙著繼續講：「……發現與埃德加・阿瑟林一

起親自去迎接威廉，並授予他皇冠是明智的。威廉的行為舉止起初還有點分寸，可是他那諾曼第人的傲慢……」說到這裡，牠突然轉向愛麗絲問道：「你現在感覺怎麼樣了？親愛的。」

「還是溼答答的。」愛麗絲悶悶不樂地說：「你說的這些對我來說完全沒有幫助。」

「既然如此，我建議休會，並立即採取更有效的措施。」多多鳥站起來嚴肅地說。

「你講清楚一點！」小鷹說：「這麼長的字句，我連一半都沒有聽懂！還有，我不相信你自己也明白！」說完後牠低下頭偷偷笑著，其他一些鳥也跟著吃吃地笑出聲來。

「我想要說的是，」多多鳥惱怒地說：「能讓我們把濕衣服弄乾的最好辦法，就是舉辦一場決策式競賽。」

「什麼是決策式競賽？」愛麗絲問，但這並不是因為她想問，而是因為多

多多鳥說到這裡突然停住了，似乎想等別人問似的，卻偏偏沒有人想發問。

多多鳥說：「要說明它嗎？最好的方法就是我們親自做做看。」（如果你也想在冬天玩這種遊戲，我可以在這裡告訴你多多鳥是怎麼做的。）

首先，牠畫出一條比賽跑道，有點像個圓圈。「圓不圓無所謂，」牠說，然後讓大家全都沿跑道分散站好，也不用喊：「一，二，三，開始！」而是誰想開始就開始，誰想停下就停下，所以，很難知道比賽什麼時候會結束。不過，牠們跑了大約半個小時，身上差不多都乾了，多多鳥突然大喊一聲：「比賽結束了！」於是大家都氣喘吁吁地圍過來，不停地問：「誰贏了？」

這個問題，多多鳥得好好考慮一下才能回答。牠坐在那裡用一根手指頭撐著前額想了好長一段時間（就像圖畫上莎士比亞的那種姿態），此時，大家都靜靜地等待著。最後，多多鳥說：「每個人都贏了，而且都有獎品！」

「可是誰來頒發獎品呢？」大家異口同聲地問。

「當然是她啦！」多多鳥指著愛麗絲。於是，大家圍住愛麗絲，亂哄哄地

叫著：「獎品！獎品！」

愛麗絲不知所措，無可奈何地把手伸進口袋，掏出一盒糖果。真幸運，還沒被鹹水浸透，她將糖果當作獎品，分給大家。

正好一人一塊。

「可是她自己也應該有一份獎品啊！」

「那當然，」老鼠說。

多多鳥非常嚴肅地回答，「你的口袋裡還有別的東西嗎？」牠轉身問愛麗絲。

「只有一個頂針。」愛麗絲傷心地說。

「把它交給我。」多多鳥說。

於是，大家又圍住了愛麗絲，多多鳥接過頂針後，又莊嚴神聖地遞給了她，說道：「我們請求你接受這枚精緻的頂針。」簡短的致辭一結束，大家全都歡呼起來。

愛麗絲認為整件事情非常荒唐，可是牠們看上去那麼一本正經，她也不敢笑，一時間又想不出有什麼話要說，只好鞠了個躬，盡可能擺出一臉莊重的樣子，伸手接過頂針。

接下來是吃糖果，這又引起一陣喧鬧，大鳥們抱怨說還沒嘗到甜味糖就沒了，而小鳥們卻被糖塊噎著了，還得讓人拍拍牠們的背。不管怎麼說總算吃完了，接下來牠們又圍成一個大圓圈坐下來，請求老鼠再跟牠們說些什麼。

「你記得嗎，你答應過要告訴我你的過去的，」愛麗絲說：「以及你為什麼討厭……討厭咪咪和汪汪。」她悄聲說完最後一句，生怕又再次得罪老鼠。

「我的委屈很長很慘。」老鼠轉向愛麗絲，嘆息著說。

愛麗絲沒有聽清楚，她看著老鼠的尾巴納悶地說：「你的尾巴的確很長啊，為什麼會說尾巴很慘呢？」（愛麗絲把「委屈」聽成「尾巴」）。在老鼠滔滔不絕說著時，愛麗絲一直為這個問題納悶，因此，在她腦中，她把故事想像成這個樣子了：

惡狗對牠在屋裡遇到的老鼠說：

「跟我到法庭去，我要控告你。

來吧，我不聽辯解，一定得審判你。

因為今天早上，我實在沒事做。」

老鼠對那無賴說：

「這樣的審判，親愛的先生，

既沒有陪審團也沒有法官，

只是白白浪費時間。」

「我就是陪審團，我就是法官，」

狡猾的老狗說：

「我要負責整個案件，

把你判處死刑。」

「你沒有注意在聽！」老鼠嚴厲地對愛麗絲說：「你在想什麼啊？」

「對不起！」愛麗絲理虧地說，「我想，你已經拐到第五個彎了吧！」

「我沒有彎！」老鼠非常生氣地厲聲說。

「你要碗（彎）啊！」愛麗絲說，她總是熱於助人，隨時準備出力，於是

焦急地四處尋找，「喔，那我幫你找找看。」

「我不吃你這一套，你的這些廢話侮辱了我！」老鼠說著站起來就走。

「我不是故意的！可是你也太容易生氣了！」可憐的愛麗絲辯解著說。

老鼠咕嚕了一聲，沒理會她。

「請你回來，把故事講完！」愛麗絲在牠背後喊著，其他人也都齊聲應和：「是啊！請回來吧！」

「牠走了，多遺憾哪！」但是，老鼠只是不耐煩地搖著腦袋，越走越快。

「牠走了，多遺憾哪！」老鼠的身影一消失，鸚鵡就嘆息著說。一隻老螃蟹趁機對女兒說：「喔，我的寶貝，你要引以為戒，以後不要亂發脾氣。」

「別說了，媽！你這麼囉嗦連牡蠣都會不耐煩。」

「要是我的黛娜在這裡就好了！」愛麗絲自言自語地大聲說：「她一定會馬上把牠抓回來的！」

小螃蟹耍著小脾氣說。

「請榮我冒昧詢問，黛娜是誰？」鸚鵡問。

愛麗絲熱切地回答，她隨時都樂意談論自己心愛的小寶貝：「黛娜是我的貓，她抓老鼠的本事可是一流的，你簡直無法想像。嘿，要是你們能看到她抓鳥的本領就好了。她只要看見鳥，一眨眼的工夫就會把牠吃到肚子裡去了！」

這話引起大家一陣恐慌，有幾隻鳥急急忙忙飛開了，一隻老喜鵲小心翼翼地把自己裹緊，特別解釋道：「我真的必須回家了，夜晚的涼氣對我的嗓子不好。」一隻金絲鳥顫抖地喊著牠的孩子們：「走吧！寶貝，你們早就該睡覺了。」牠們都找各種藉口離開了。不久又只剩下愛麗絲孤零零一個人了。

「真後悔又提起黛娜！」愛麗絲傷心地自言自語，「這裡好像沒有一個喜歡她的，唉！只有我知道牠是世界上最好的貓！啊，我親愛的黛娜，真不知道什麼時候才能再見到你！」說到這裡，可憐的小愛麗絲哭了起來，她非常孤獨和沮喪。然而，過了一會兒，她又聽見不遠處傳來了腳步聲。她心中期待是那隻老鼠改變了主意，回來繼續講牠的故事。

想一想

你也常常需要參加「競賽」嗎？你覺得你遇到的競賽比較好玩還是多多鳥的決策式競賽？

第四章　兔子派出小比爾

原來是那隻小白兔又慢慢地走回來了，邊走邊焦急地四處張望，好像在找什麼東西似的。愛麗絲還聽到牠低聲嘀咕著：「公爵夫人啊！公爵夫人，唉！我親愛的小爪子呀！我的小鬍子呀！她肯定會把我處死的，一定的！就像雪貂是雪貂那樣千真萬確！我到底把它們丟到哪裡去了？」這時愛麗絲馬上猜到牠正在找那把扇子和那雙羊皮手套，於是她也好心地到處尋找，但是都找不到，自從她在池子裡游泳之後，好像一切都變得不一樣了，那個大廳、那個玻璃桌子都已消失得無影無蹤。

過了一會兒，當愛麗絲還在到處尋找的時候，兔子看見她，狠狠地對她嚷道：「瑪麗安，你在這裡幹嘛？趕快回家給我拿一雙手套和一把扇子來。趕快

去！」愛麗絲嚇壞了，顧不得向牠解釋牠認錯人，趕緊照牠所指的方向跑去。

「牠把我當成牠的女僕了，」她一邊跑，一邊對自己說：「等牠發現我是誰一定會嚇一跳的！不過，我最好還是幫牠把手套和扇子拿來——要是我能找到的話。」說著，她看到一幢精緻的小房子，門上掛著一塊發亮的黃銅小牌子，上面刻著「白兔先生」。她沒有敲門就走進去，急忙往樓上跑，生怕碰上真的瑪麗安，如果那樣的話，在還沒有找到手套和扇子前她就會被趕出去。

「真奇怪！」愛麗絲自言自語地說：「竟然幫一隻兔子跑腿，我看下一次就會輪到黛娜使喚我了。」她開始想像那種情景：「『愛麗絲小姐，立刻到這裡來，你得準備去散步了。』『馬上就來，保姆！不過在黛娜回來之前，我還得守著這個老鼠洞，不許老鼠出來。』不過，要是黛娜像這樣使喚人的話，他們肯定不會讓她待在家裡的。」她繼續這樣想著。

這時候，她已經走進一間整潔的小房間，窗邊有張小桌子，正像她所希望的那樣，桌上有一把扇子和兩、三雙白羔羊皮小手套。她拿起扇子和一雙手

套，正要離開房間，忽然看到鏡子前有一個小瓶子。這次瓶子上沒有寫著「喝我」，然而她還是拔開瓶塞就往嘴裡倒。她對自己說：「不管我吃了或喝了什麼東西，總會發生有趣的事。所以我要看看這一瓶能把我怎麼樣。我真希望它會讓我變大。說真的，老是這麼小真是煩死了。」

果然如她所願，而且速度比她預期的還要快，半瓶還沒有喝完，頭就頂到了天花板，她只得彎下身體，免得把脖子擠斷了。

愛麗絲趕緊扔掉瓶子，對自己說：「這樣就已經夠了，不要再長了，可是就算是現在這樣，我也已經出不去了。唉！要是剛才沒喝那麼多就好了！」

後悔已經太遲了，她繼續長啊，長啊，沒多久就只能跪在地板上了，很快地連跪的地方都沒了，她只得躺下，一隻手臂撐在地上，一隻手臂抱著頭。可是還在長，實在沒有辦法，她只得把一隻手臂伸出窗子，一隻腳伸進煙囪裡，然後自言自語：「再長下去的話，我也沒有辦法了，我會變成什麼樣子呢？」

幸運的是這個小魔術瓶的法力已經發揮完了，她不再長大了，可是心裡卻高興不起來，因為看來她再也沒有機會從這個房子裡出去了。

「還是在家裡好，」可憐的愛麗絲想，「在家裡不會一會下子變大，一會下子變小，更不會被老鼠和兔子使喚。我真後悔鑽進這個兔子洞，可是……可是這裡的生活是這麼的稀奇古怪，我真不知道還有什麼事會發生在我身上。以前讀童話故事時，總認為那種事情絕不可能會發生，現在自己卻來到童話世界裡了。應該寫一本關於我的書，應該有一本，等我長大了，我要寫一本——

可是我現在已經長大了啊！」她又傷心地加了一句：「至少這裡已經沒有地方可以再讓我長大了。」

「可是，話說回來，」愛麗絲想：「我不會比現在年齡更大了！這倒是個安慰，我永遠不會成為老太婆。但是又得一直上學了。唉，我可不喜歡！」

「哎呀，你這個傻愛麗絲！」她回答自己：「在這裡要怎麼上學呢？這間房子幾乎都裝不下你了，哪裡還有地方可以放書呢？」

她就這樣繼續自己和自己辯論著，先裝成這個人問，然後又裝成另一個人回答，說了一大堆話。但是，幾分鐘後，她聽到門外有說話的聲音，於是她停止對話仔細聆聽。

「瑪麗安，瑪麗安！」聲音喊道：「趕快把手套給我拿出來。」然後是一連串小腳步聲上了樓梯。愛麗絲知道是兔子來找她了，她嚇得發抖，哆嗦得屋子都搖動了，完全忘記自己現在已經比兔子大了一千倍，根本不用怕牠。

轉眼間兔子到了門口，試著想推開門，但門是朝裡面開的，愛麗絲的手臂

肘正好頂著門，兔子推也推不動，愛麗絲聽到牠自言自語說：「那麼我繞過去，從窗子爬進去。」

「那樣你還是進不來的。」愛麗絲想。等了一會兒，直到她聽到兔子已走到窗下，她突然伸出手，在空中抓了一把，什麼也沒有抓到，卻聽到摔倒後的尖叫聲，和玻璃破碎的嘩啦啦響聲，她猜想那兔子大概掉進溫室的玻璃天窗下，或者什麼類似的東西裡去了。

緊接著傳來兔子氣惱的喊叫聲：「帕特！帕特！你在哪裡？」接著，是一個陌生的聲音回答：「我在這裡，正在挖蘋果樹呢，老爺！」

「哼！還挖蘋果樹呢！」兔子氣呼呼地說：「過來，把我拉出來！」又是一陣打碎玻璃的聲音。

「告訴我，帕特，窗子裡的東西是什麼？」

「啊，是一隻手臂，老爺！」（他發音發成了「手逼」。）

「一隻手臂！你這個笨蛋，誰看過這麼大的手臂，把窗戶都塞滿了！」

「沒錯，老爺，是塞滿了，但它還是一隻手臂啊！」

「好啦！別囉嗦了，不管怎樣，它都沒有理由塞在那裡，去把它拿走！」

過了半天都沒有動靜，愛麗絲只能斷斷續續地聽到幾句他們小聲的談話，例如：「我怕看見它，老爺，我真的很怕它！」……「照我的話做，你這個膽小鬼！」最後，她又張開手，在空中抓了一把，這次她聽到了兩聲尖叫和更多玻璃破碎的聲音。「這裡一定有很多種黃瓜的玻璃溫室！」愛麗絲心想，「不知道他們下一步要幹什麼？是不是要把我從窗子裡拉出去，嘿，我真希望他們能這樣做，我實在不想再待下去了！」

又過了一會兒，都沒有聽到什麼動靜，後來傳來小車輪的滾動聲，以及許多人說話的聲音：「另一個梯子在哪裡？……嗯，我只拿了一個，另一個比爾拿走了……比爾，把梯子拿過來，小伙子……這裡，放到這個角上……不，先把它們綁在一起，還不到一半高呢！……對，夠了，你別挑剔了……比爾，這裡，抓住這根繩子……屋頂承受得了嗎？……小心那塊鬆了的瓦片……哎呀！」

掉下來了！低頭！（砰的一聲巨響）……現在誰來做？……我認為比爾應該可以，牠可以從煙囪爬下去。……不，我不要！……你一定要做！……這我可不幹……應該比爾下去……比爾！老爺說一定要讓你下煙囪！」

「啊，這麼說比爾就要從煙囪下來了，」愛麗絲自言自語地說：「嘿，牠們好像把什麼事情都推到比爾身上，我可不做比爾這樣的角色。說真的這個壁爐很窄，不過我還是可以踢那麼一下。」

她把伸進煙囪裡的腳收了收，等了又等，一直聽到一個小動物（她猜不出是什麼動物）在煙囪裡連滾帶爬地靠近她的腳，於是她一邊對自己說：「這就是比爾了，」一邊往上狠狠地踢了一腳，然後等著看再來會發生什麼事。

一開始，她聽到一片叫嚷聲：「比爾飛出來啦！」然後是兔子的聲音：「喂，籬笆邊的人，快接住牠！」一下子又沒有聲音了，接著又是一片混亂的說話聲：「扶起牠的頭……快，白蘭地……別嗆著牠了！現在怎麼樣了？老兄，你碰見了什麼？快告訴我們！」

等了一會兒，聽見一個細微、短促的聲音，（「是比爾！」愛麗絲心想。）「唔，我根本搞不清楚，……我不喝了，謝謝你們。現在我好多了……不過我心裡慌亂得很，沒辦法對你們細說——我只記得，有個像彈簧玩具一樣的東西向我衝過來，然後我就像火箭一樣飛了出來！」

「沒錯，老兄！你真的像火箭一樣！」其他的聲音應著。

「我們必須燒了那棟房子！」這是兔子的聲音。愛麗絲一聽，拚命地放聲高喊：「你們敢，我就放黛娜出來咬你們！」

突然間一片鴉雀無聲，愛麗絲想：「不知道他們下一步要幹什麼！如果有點頭腦的話，就該把屋頂拆掉。」過了一、兩分鐘，他們又開始跑來跑去，愛麗絲聽到那兔子說：「先用一桶試試。」

「一桶什麼呢？」愛麗絲心裡正在猜測時，小卵石就像像暴雨般地從窗子扔進來了，有些還打在她臉上，「我得想辦法讓他們住手，」她自言自語地說，然後大聲喊道：「你們最好別再這樣做了！」接著又是一陣鴉雀無聲。

就在這時，愛麗絲驚訝地發現，那些小卵石掉到地板上都變成了小蛋糕，她腦子裡立刻閃過了一個聰明的念頭：「如果我吃上一塊，可能會讓我變小，既然現在我已經不可能更大了，那麼，它一定會把我變小的。」

於是，她吞下一塊蛋糕，果然立刻就縮小了。她索性再吃，直到恰好縮小到能夠穿過門的時候，就立刻跑出那棟房子，一出來就發現一大群小動物和小鳥都在外面等著，那隻可憐的小蜥蜴——比爾，就在其中，被兩隻豚鼠扶著喝一瓶藥水。愛麗絲一出現，牠們全都衝了上來。但她拚命地跑，總算跑走，不久後就平安地進入一個茂密的樹林。

「我要做的第一件事，」愛麗絲一邊在樹林中漫步一邊自言自語：「就是找到可以通往那個可愛小花園的路。這把自己變回正常的大小，而第二件就是是我最好的計畫了。」

聽起來，這個計畫好像還不錯，安

排得相當美妙而簡單，但唯一的困難在於她根本不知道怎樣才能做到。正當她在樹林中著急地四處張望時，頭上忽然傳來一聲尖銳的狗叫聲。她趕緊抬起頭往上看，一隻巨大的幼犬，正瞪著又大又圓的眼睛看著她，還輕輕地伸出一隻爪子要抓她。「可憐的小東西！」愛麗絲用哄小孩的聲調說，一邊還努力地向牠吹口哨。可是一想到牠可能是餓了，愛麗絲心裡就嚇得要死，要真是那樣的話，不管她再怎麼哄牠，牠還是很有可能會把她吃掉。

愛麗絲下意識地拾起一根小樹枝，

伸向小狗，那隻小狗立刻跳了起來，高興地注注叫著，撲向樹枝要咬，愛麗絲急忙躲進一排薊樹叢後面，免得被小狗撞倒。她剛從樹叢的另一邊探出頭來，小狗又朝樹枝撲了過來。牠衝得太急了，不但沒有抓到樹枝，反而翻了個筋斗；愛麗絲覺得像是在和一匹馬玩耍，隨時都有被踩到的危險，於是就繞著薊樹叢跑了起來。那隻小狗又一陣一陣地衝向樹枝，每一次都衝過了頭，然後再遠遠地後退，嘴裡不停地狂吠。最後，牠在很遠的地方蹲坐下來，伸出舌頭大口地喘氣，一雙大眼睛也半閉上了。

這是愛麗絲逃跑的最好機會，於是她轉身就跑，跑得上氣不接下氣，直到小狗的叫聲聽起來也很遠了，才停了下來。

「不過那真是一隻可愛的小狗！」愛麗絲靠在一棵毛茛樹上休息，還拿了一片毛茛葉當葉子。「要是我像正常時那樣的大小，我真想教牠玩許多把戲！啊，天哪，我差點忘記了自己還要想辦法再長大！讓我想一想，怎麼辦才好呢？我想我得吃或喝點什麼東西，可是該吃點或喝點什麼呢？」

最大的問題當然是「什麼東西？」愛麗絲看著周圍的花草，看不出有什麼東西像是可以拿來吃喝的。她身旁長著一棵巨大的蘑菇，差不多和她一樣高。

她往它底下看看，再往它後面和兩邊看看，想到還應該看看上面有什麼東西。

她踮起腳尖，伸長脖子，沿著蘑菇的邊緣往上看，正好與一隻大毛毛蟲的目光相遇，那隻毛毛蟲交叉著手臂坐在蘑菇頂上，一聲不吭地抽著一支長長的水煙管，完全不理愛麗絲。

想一想

為什麼大家都把麻煩的事情推給比爾？如果不想當比爾的話，應該要怎麼拒絕兔子無理的請求？

057　第四章　兔子派出小比爾

第五章　毛毛蟲的忠告

毛毛蟲和愛麗絲彼此一聲不吭地對視了好一會兒。最後，毛毛蟲從嘴裡取出水煙管，慢吞吞地、無精打采地開了口。

「你是誰呀？」毛毛蟲問道。

這可不像是引人談話的開場白，愛麗絲有點不好意思地回答說：「我……現在很難說，先生……至少今天起床時我還知道自己是誰的，但從那之後，我就變來變去變了好幾回。」

「你這話是什麼意思？」毛毛蟲嚴厲地說：「給我說清楚點！」

「我怕自己沒辦法解釋清楚，先生，」愛麗絲說：「因為現在我已經不是自己了，你看。」

「我看不出來。」毛毛蟲說。

「我實在無法再解釋得更清楚了，」愛麗絲彬彬有禮地回答：「因為我自己也搞不懂是怎麼回事；而且，一天裡變了好幾次，真叫人糊塗。」

「一點都不糊塗。」毛毛蟲說。

「唉，也許你現在還沒有辦法體會，」愛麗絲說：「可是當你必須變成一個蝶蛹時——你要知道你總有一天會這樣的——然後再變成一隻蝴蝶，我想你一定會感到有點奇怪，是不是？」

「完全不會。」毛毛蟲說。

「喔！也許你的感覺和我的不一樣，」愛麗絲說：「可是那些事對我來說真的非常非常奇怪。」

「那你呢！」毛毛蟲輕蔑地說：「你是誰？」

這個問題又將他們帶回談話的開頭，對於毛毛蟲過於簡短的回答，愛麗絲開始有點不高興，她挺直身體嚴肅地說道：「我想你應該先告訴我你是誰。」

「為什麼？」毛毛蟲說。

這又是一個令人困惑的難題，愛麗絲想不出合適的原因來回答，而毛毛蟲看起來很不高興的樣子，因此愛麗絲掉頭就走了。

「回來！」毛毛蟲在她身後喊道：「我有重要的話要說！」

這話聽起來倒是滿吸引人的，於是愛麗絲又回來了。

「要控制自己的脾氣。」毛毛蟲說。

「你要講的就是這個？」愛麗絲盡力忍住了怒氣發問。

「不。」毛毛蟲說。

愛麗絲心想，既然沒有別的事，不如就在這裡等一等，也許牠終究會說出一些值得聽的話。有好幾分鐘，毛毛蟲只顧著悶頭吞雲吐霧不說話。最後牠鬆開手臂，把水煙管從嘴裡拿出來，說道：「你認為你已經變了，是嗎？」

「我想是的，先生。」愛麗絲說。「我平時記得的事現在都想不起來了，而且連保持同樣的身材十分鐘都做不到。」

「你想不起來什麼？」毛毛蟲問。

「我試著背《忙碌小蜜蜂怎麼樣了》，可是背出來的完全變了樣！」愛麗絲用非常沮喪的口氣回答。

「那你背一背《你已經老了，威廉爸爸》。」毛毛蟲說。

愛麗絲雙手交叉，開始背誦：

年輕的男孩說：「你已經老了，威廉爸爸，你的頭髮白得差不多了，可是你還老是倒立著──你想想，你這歲數，合適嗎？」

「年輕的時候，」威廉爸爸回答兒子說：

「我怕腦子會受傷：可是現在我能肯定自己沒腦子了，

所以，我就一遍一遍這樣玩。」

年輕的男孩說：「像我剛剛說過的，你已經老了，

而且胖得出奇；

可是你一個跟斗從門口到著翻進來，

請問，這是什麼道理？」

「年輕的時候，」老哲人邊說邊晃著灰白的捲髮，

「我讓四肢保持十分靈巧

全靠使用這種油膏——五塊錢一盒——

還是我賣你兩罐怎麼樣？」

「你已經老了，」年輕的男孩說：

「下巴已經衰弱得

比牛板油硬的你都咬不動；

可你卻把一整隻鵝連喙帶骨頭全都吃光——

請問你是怎麼辦到的？」

「年輕的時候，」爸爸說：

「我研讀的是法律，

我和我的妻子辯論每個案例，

因此我的下巴肌肉練得非常發達

在我後半輩子還堅韌有力。」

「你已經老了，」年輕的男孩說：「幾乎沒人認為

你的目光會如從前般堅定；

可是你卻能讓鰻魚在鼻尖上豎立，

是什麼使你如此聰明絕頂？」

「我回答了三個問題，已經很多了啦！」

父親說：「你不要太超過！

難道你以為我會整天聽你講這些有的沒的？

你快點離開，不然我一腳把你踹到樓下！」

「背錯了。」毛毛蟲說。

「恐怕不全對，」愛麗絲心虛地說：「有些詞已經改了。」

「從頭到尾都錯了。」毛毛蟲乾脆地說。接著他們沉默了許久。

「你想變成多大呢？」毛毛蟲先開口。

「唉！多大我倒不在乎。」愛麗絲連忙回答：「可是，一個人總不會喜歡

老是變來變去的，這你是知道的。」

「我不知道。」毛毛蟲說。

愛麗絲什麼也沒說，長這麼大從不曾被人這樣不斷反駁，她覺得自己都快要發脾氣了。

「你滿意現在的樣子嗎？」毛毛蟲問。

「喔，先生，我希望能再大一點，如果你不介意的話。」愛麗絲說：「只有七公分高，實在太不像樣了。」

「這是一個非常合適的高度。」毛毛蟲生氣地說，還把身體挺直豎起來

（他恰好七公分高）。

「可是我不習慣這個高度！」愛麗絲可憐兮兮地說道，心裡想著：「但願這傢伙別發火！」

「久了就會習慣的！」毛毛蟲說完又把水煙管放進嘴裡抽起來了。

這次，愛麗絲耐心地等著牠開口。過了一、兩分鐘後，毛毛蟲從嘴裡拿出

水煙管，打了一、兩個呵欠，身體搖了搖，然後從蘑菇上下來，向草叢爬去。

離開時順口說道：「一邊會使你長高，另一邊會使你變矮。」

「什麼東西的一邊，什麼東西的另一邊？」愛麗絲想著。

「蘑菇。」毛毛蟲說，像是能聽到愛麗絲心中的疑問一樣。轉眼間毛毛蟲就不見了。

愛麗絲待在那，端詳著那個蘑菇，想弄清楚是哪兩邊。可是蘑菇圓溜溜的，愛麗絲發現這真是個難題。不管怎樣，她後來還是伸開雙臂環抱著蘑菇，而且盡量伸得遠一些，然後兩隻手分別掰下蘑菇的兩邊。

「可是現在哪邊是哪邊呢？」她問自己，然後咬了右手那塊試試看。才吃到嘴裡，就覺得下巴被猛烈地碰了一下：原來下巴已經碰到腳背了。

突然的變化使她嚇了一跳，縮得太快了，再不抓緊時間就完了，於是，她馬上又去吃另一塊，雖然下巴和腳頂得太緊，嘴巴幾乎要張不開了，但她還是啃了一點左手的另一塊蘑菇。

「啊，我的頭終於自由了！」愛麗絲高興地說，可是轉眼間又恐懼了起來。因為，她發現自己的手臂不見了。她往下看的時候，只見到長得不得了的脖子，像是聳立在綠色海洋中的高聳草稈。

「那一大片綠色東西是什麼呢？」愛麗絲說：「我的肩膀呢？啊！我可憐的雙手，我怎麼看不見你們？」她說話的時候揮動雙手，可是除了遠處的樹叢中出現一些顫動外，什麼動靜也沒有。

看起來，她已經沒辦法把手舉到頭上了，於是，她打算把頭彎下去靠近她的手。她高興地發現自己的脖子像條大蛇一樣，能夠輕而易舉地上下左右扭動，她將脖子朝下，變成一個 Z 字形，準備鑽到綠葉叢中。她發現這些綠色海洋不是別的東西，正是她剛才徘徊的林子的樹梢。此時，一陣尖利的嘶聲讓她慌忙縮回頭。一隻巨大的鴿子飛到她臉上，揮著翅膀瘋狂地撲打她。

「蛇！」鴿子尖叫著。

「我不是蛇！」愛麗絲生氣地說：「走開！」

「蛇！我說就是蛇！」鴿子重複，但口氣比剛才溫和多了，然後啜泣著加了一句：「我想盡了各種方法，牠們就是不放過我！」

「你在說什麼呀，我都聽不懂！」愛麗絲說。

「我試過了樹根，試過了岸邊，也試過了籬笆，」鴿子繼續說著，並沒有注意她，「可是這些大蛇！牠們真是貪心不足！」

愛麗絲越來越糊塗了，但是她知道，在鴿子說完自己的話之前，她說什麼都是沒有用的。

「就好像嫌孵蛋還不夠麻煩似的，」鴿子說：「我還得日夜提防那些大蛇，天哪！整整三個星期我都沒闔過眼呢！」

「真不幸，你被人家擾亂得不得安寧。」愛麗絲說，她似乎開始有點明白牠的意思了。

「我剛剛把家搬到林中最高的樹上，」鴿子繼續說，提高嗓門變成了尖聲

嘶叫，「以為已經擺脫牠們了，結果牠們還是從天上蜿蜒地蠕動著下來了。

呸，蛇！」

「告訴你，我可不是蛇！」愛麗絲說：「我是一個⋯⋯我是一個⋯⋯」

「啊，你是什麼呢？」鴿子說，「我看你還想編出什麼謊話來！」

「我⋯⋯我是一個小女孩。」經過這一天的變化，愛麗絲開始有點懷疑自己了。

「還真會說故事！」鴿子輕蔑地說：「我這輩子看過的小女孩可不少，從來沒有一個像你一樣有這麼長的脖子！沒有，絕對沒有！你就是一條蛇，否認也沒有用！我猜你接下來還打算告訴我，你從來沒有嚐過蛋的味道吧！」

「我當然吃過許多蛋，」愛麗絲說，她是個非常誠實的孩子。「你要知道，小女孩吃的蛋可不比蛇吃的少。」

「我才不相信你呢，」鴿子說，「如果她們也吃蛋的話，那她們也是蛇的一種。」

這對於愛麗絲而言可真是前所未聞，她愣了幾分鐘。於是鴿子趁機加了一句：「反正你是在找蛋，這一點我一清二楚，因此，不管你是小女孩還是蛇，對我來說都一樣。」

「但這對我很不一樣，」愛麗絲急忙分辯，「老實說，我根本就不是在找蛋，就算我是在找蛋，我也不會要你的蛋！我從來不吃生蛋的。」

「哼，那你就滾開！」鴿子生氣說著，又飛下去鑽進自己的窩裡。愛麗絲使勁往樹林裡蹲，可是她的脖子常被樹枝纏住，不得不隨時停下來清理一番。

過了一會兒，她想起手裡還捏著的兩塊蘑菇，她小心地咬咬這塊，又咬咬那塊，於是她一會兒長高，一會兒變矮，最後終於使自己恢復到平常的高度了。

由於很久沒有處於正常高度，起初感覺很奇怪，不過幾分鐘後就習慣了，她又開始像往常一樣自言自語。「好啦，現在我的計畫完成一半了。這些變化是多麼奇怪啊！我簡直無從得知下一分鐘自己會是什麼樣子。不管怎樣，現在我總算恢復原來的大小了，下一步要做的就是去那個美麗花園。我該怎麼做

呢？」說著說著她來到了一片寬廣的空地，那裡有一棟一百二十公分高的小房子。「不管誰住在這裡，」愛麗絲心想，「我現在這樣的個頭碰見他們，都會把他們的魂都給嚇掉。」於是，她咬了一點右手上的蘑菇，直到縮小成二十公分高，才敢向那棟小房子走去。

你覺得詩中那位威廉爸爸是個怎麼樣的人？你曾經遇過像他一樣的大人嗎？

第六章　豬與胡椒

愛麗絲站在小房子前看了一、兩分鐘，琢磨著下一步該做些什麼。突然一個穿著制服的僕人（她之所以會認為他是僕人，是因為他穿著僕人的制服，如果只看臉的話，會把他看成一條魚）從樹林跑出來，用指關節使勁地敲著門。另一個同樣穿著制服，長著圓圓的臉龐和青蛙一樣大眼睛的僕人開了門。愛麗絲注意到這兩個僕

人都戴著塗了脂粉的捲髮。她十分好奇，很想知道到底是怎麼回事，於是從樹林裡悄悄探出頭來偷聽。

那位魚臉僕人從手臂下拿出一封幾乎和自己一樣大的信，把它遞給另一個僕人，並用嚴肅的語氣說：「呈給公爵夫人，這是皇后邀請她去玩槌球的邀請函。」那位蛙臉僕人改變了一下句子的排列順序，用同樣嚴肅的語氣重複了一遍：「這是皇后的邀請函，請公爵夫人去玩槌球。」

然後兩人朝彼此深深地鞠了躬，結果他們的捲髮都纏在一起了。

愛麗絲看到這個情景，忍不住笑了出來，為了不被他們聽見，她不得不遠遠地跑進樹林裡。過了一會兒再出來偷看時，魚臉僕人已經走了，另一位則坐在門口的地上，愣愣地望著天空發呆。

愛麗絲怯生生地走到門口，敲了敲門。

「敲門也沒用，」蛙臉僕人說：「有兩個原因。第一，因爲我和你一樣都在門外；第二，他們在裡面吵吵鬧鬧的，根本聽不到敲門聲。」的確，裡面傳來的吵鬧聲可眞不小——又是嚎叫聲，又是打噴嚏聲，不時還夾雜著打破東西的聲音，好像是盤子或者瓷壺之類的東西。

「那麼，請告訴我，」愛麗絲說：「要怎樣才能進去呢？」

「如果這扇門是在你和我之間，那麼你敲門可能還有意義，」僕人根本沒有理會愛麗絲，繼續自言自語：「譬如你在裡面敲門，你知道的，我就能讓你出來。」他說話時，兩眼一直盯著天空，愛麗絲覺得這樣很沒禮貌。「不過也許他也沒有辦法，」她對自己說：「他的眼睛都快長到頭頂上了。然而無論如何，他至少可以回答問題的……我要怎樣才能進去呢？」她提高嗓門，又問了一次。

「我打算坐在這裡，」那僕人繼續說他的，「一直到明天……」

這時，房門開了，一個大盤子朝著僕人的頭飛來，掠過他的鼻子，砸在他身後的一棵樹上，碎了。

「……或者後天。」僕人繼續用同樣的口吻說，就好像什麼都沒有發生過似的。

「我該怎麼進去呢？」愛麗絲又問一遍，聲音更大了。

「你一定要進去嗎？」蛙臉僕人說：「你要知道，這是首要問題。」

他說的話倒是沒錯，不過愛麗絲不喜歡他對她說話的口氣。「真讓人受不了，」她嘟囔著，「這些傢伙討論問題的方法簡直叫人發瘋！」

那僕人似乎認為這是重複自己的話的好機會，不過他稍微改變了一下說法：「我打算從早到晚一直坐在這裡，坐坐走走，走走坐坐，一天又一天地坐下去。」

「可是我該做什麼呢？」愛麗絲說。

「隨便你，你想幹什麼就幹什麼。」蛙臉僕人說完就吹起口哨來了。

「唉，跟他說話一點用也沒有！」愛麗絲失望地說：「他根本就是一個白癡！」然後她就自己推開門進去了。

大門直通一間大廚房，整間廚房都煙霧騰騰的。公爵夫人坐在房子中間一把三腳小椅子上，手裡抱著一個小孩。女廚師靠著爐子邊，在一口大鍋裡攪拌著，鍋裡好像盛滿了湯。

「湯裡的胡椒一定是放得太多了！」愛麗絲對自己說，不停地打著噴嚏。

空氣裡的胡椒味確實太濃了，連公爵夫人也不時打上幾個噴嚏。至於那個嬰兒，不是打噴嚏就是大哭，一刻也停不下來。廚房裡沒有打噴嚏的只有那位女廚師和一隻大貓，那隻貓正趴在爐子旁咧著大嘴笑著。

「請問，」愛麗絲有點膽怯地問，因為她還不太確定自己應不應該先開口，「為什麼你的貓會那樣咧著嘴笑呢？」

「牠是柴郡貓，」公爵夫人說：「所以才會笑。豬！」

最後那個字說得相當兇狠，嚇了愛麗絲一大跳。不過，她馬上發現那是衝

著小孩說的，並不是針對自己，於是她又鼓起了勇氣，繼續說：「我還不知道柴郡貓總是這樣笑，眞的，我從來就不知道貓會笑。」

「牠們都會，」公爵夫人說：「起碼大多數都會笑的。」

「我連一隻都沒見過。」愛麗絲非常客氣地說，爲自己和她變談得來感到高興。

「你太孤陋寡聞了，」公爵夫人說：「這是事實。」

愛麗絲不喜歡這句話的口氣，心想最好還是換個話題。正想著的時候，女廚師把湯鍋從火上端開，之後隨即拿起手邊能構得到的所有東西砸向公爵夫人和嬰兒。先是鉗子，然後是平底鍋、盆子、盤子，一個個像暴風雨似地飛過來。公爵夫人毫不理會，甚至打到身上都沒反應。至於那嬰兒，因爲他本來就哭得就很兇，也看不出來這些東西是不是打到他了。

「喔，拜託你小心一點！」愛麗絲嚇壞了，拚命地喊著，「喔，他的小鼻子完蛋了。」說話時，一個特大號的平底鍋緊擦著小嬰兒的鼻子飛過，差點就

把他的鼻子削掉了。

「如果每個人都不管別人的閒事，」公爵夫人嘶啞著嗓子嚷著：「地球就會比現在轉得快多了。」

「這倒不見得有什麼好處，」愛麗絲說，她很高興能有個機會好展示一下自己的知識，「想想看，這會給白天和黑夜帶來什麼影響呢？要知道地球繞地軸轉一圈要二十四個小時——」

「說什麼地軸，」公爵夫人說：「把她的頭砍掉！」

愛麗絲非常擔心地看了女廚師

一眼，看看她有沒有聽到這個命令，但女廚師正忙著攪湯，好像根本沒聽到，

於是愛麗絲又繼續說：「我想是二十四個小時，要是十二個小時，我……」

「喔，少煩我了！」公爵夫人說：「我最受不了數字了！」說著又照顧孩

子去了，她唱著某種搖籃曲，每唱一句就猛搖孩子幾下……

對你的小孩子要粗聲粗氣，

只要他一打噴嚏就揍他；

他這麼做只不過是為了要搗蛋，

因為他知道這很惹人厭。

合唱

哇喔！哇喔！哇喔！

（女廚和那小嬰兒也加了進來）……

公爵夫人唱到第二段時，用力地把小嬰兒丟上丟下，那可憐的小傢伙哭得更兇了，以至於愛麗絲幾乎都聽不清楚歌詞：

我嚴厲地對我的小傢伙説話，

他一打噴嚏我就揍他；

因為只要他願意，

就可以好好享受胡椒味啦！

合唱

哇喔！哇喔！哇喔！

「過來！如果你願意的話，你可以抱他一會兒！」公爵夫人說完就把小孩扔給她，「我要去和皇后玩槌球了，我得準備一下。」她邊說邊急忙地走出房

間。女廚師把一口油鍋對著她的後腦扔

過去，但沒打到。

　　愛麗絲費力地接住那個小孩，因為

他是個樣子奇特的小東西，手臂和腿向

四面八方伸展，「真像隻海星。」愛麗

絲想著。她接住他時，可憐的小傢伙像

蒸汽機一樣地噴氣，一會兒蜷曲起來，

一會兒又伸展開，就這樣不停地折騰了

一、兩分鐘，弄得愛麗絲費盡力氣才勉

強把他抓住。

　　等她好不容易找到一種抱住他的辦

法時（像打結一樣把他纏在一起，然後

抓緊他的右耳和左腳，就不會再鬆開

），她把他帶到屋子外面的空地。「如果我不把這嬰兒帶走，」愛麗絲心想，「她們肯定一、兩天就會把他弄死的。把他扔下不管豈不是和殺人一樣嗎？」她大聲說出最後那句話，小傢伙咕嚕了一聲作為回答（這時他已經不打噴嚏了）。「你不要這樣咕嚕咕嚕的，」愛麗絲說：「這不是好孩子說話該有的樣子。」

嬰兒又咕嚕了一聲，愛麗絲很著急地看了看他的臉，想知道是怎麼回事。只見他鼻子朝天，根本不像人的鼻子，倒像個豬鼻子；那兩隻眼睛也太小了，根本不像是孩子的眼睛。總之，愛麗絲一點也不喜歡他這副模樣。「也許是因為他在哭吧，」愛麗絲想。於是她又看了看他的眼睛，瞧瞧有沒有眼淚。

沒有，並沒有眼淚。「如果你變成豬，」愛麗絲嚴肅地說：「聽著，我就不理你了！」那可憐的小傢伙又哭了一聲（或者說又咕嚕了一聲，很難說到底是哪種），然後他們一聲不吭地走了一會兒。

愛麗絲正想著：「把這小傢伙帶回家裡該怎麼辦才好？」他又大聲地咕嚕

了起來，愛麗絲馬上警覺地看了看他的臉。這次一點都沒錯，他不折不扣就是一頭豬。這時她覺得如果再抱著他就太可笑了。

於是，她把那小東西放下來，看著他很快地跑進樹林去，才如釋重負地鬆了口氣。「如果他長大的話，」愛麗絲自言自語地說：「一定會變成很可怕的樣子，不過如果是豬的話，倒是一頭漂亮的豬。」然後，她把自己認識的孩子一個個想了一遍，看看誰如果變成豬會更像樣些，她才剛想對自己說：「如果有人知道正確的變身方式的話──」忽然，她發現那隻柴郡貓正坐在幾公尺遠的樹枝上，嚇了她一跳。

那隻貓看見愛麗絲，只是咧著嘴笑，「樣子看起來倒很親切。」愛麗絲想，不過牠還是有很長的爪子和那些牙齒，應該對牠尊敬點。

「柴郡貓，」她怯生生地開口。因為她還不清楚牠喜歡不喜歡這個名字，

然而，牠的嘴咧得更大了一些。「喔，牠很高興。」愛麗絲想，然後接著說：

「請您告訴我，我應該走哪條路？」

「這要看你想去哪裡，」貓說。

「去哪裡我都不太在乎。」愛麗絲說。

「那你走哪條路都沒關係。」貓說。

「只要……我能走到一個地方。」愛麗絲又補充說了一句。

「喔，那當然，」貓說：「只要你走得夠遠，一定能走到一個地方。」

愛麗絲覺得他說的話沒錯，於是試著問其他問題：「這附近都住些什麼樣的人？」

「那邊，」貓說著，右爪子揮了一圈，「住著一位帽匠。而那邊，」貓又揮動另一隻爪子，「住著一隻三月兔。你喜歡拜訪誰就拜訪誰，他們兩個都是瘋子。」

「可是我不想到一群瘋子中間去。」愛麗絲回答。

「喔，這沒有辦法啊，」貓說：「這裡的全都是瘋子，我是瘋子，你也是瘋子。」

「你怎麼知道我瘋了？」愛麗絲問。

「一定的啊，」貓說：「不然你就不會到這裡來了。」

愛麗絲認為這個理由一點都不充分，不過她還是接著問：「那你又是怎麼知道自己是瘋子呢？」

「應該吧，」愛麗絲說。

「好，首先，」貓說：「狗不是瘋子，這你同意吧？」

「好，那麼，」貓接著說：「你看，狗生氣就汪汪叫，高興就搖尾巴，可是我呢，高興就狂吠，生氣就搖尾巴。所以，我是瘋子。」

「你那是喵喵叫，不是狂吠。」愛麗絲說。

「隨你怎麼說，」貓說：「你今天和皇后一起玩槌球嗎？」

「我倒是很喜歡玩槌球遊戲，」愛麗絲說：「可是到現在還沒有人邀請我呢！」

「你會在那裡看到我，」說完貓就突然消失了。

愛麗絲對此並不太驚奇，她已經見怪不怪了。她看了看貓剛才坐過的地方，發現貓又突然出現了。

「喔對了，那個嬰兒變成什麼了？」貓說：「我差點就忘了問。」

「變成一隻豬了。」愛麗絲平靜地回答說，就好像貓再次出現是正常的事。

「跟我想的一樣。」貓說著又消失了。

愛麗絲等了一會兒，希望能再看見牠，可是牠再也沒有出現。於是，過了一、兩分鐘，她朝著三月兔住的方向走去。「帽匠嘛，我以前見過的。」她對自己說：「三月兔一定有趣得多，而且現在是五月，也許牠不至於瘋得太厲害——至少不會像三月的時候那麼瘋吧！」就在她說這些話的同時，她的眼睛往上一瞄，又看見那隻貓坐在一根樹枝上。

「你剛才說的是豬，還是樹？」貓問。

「我說的是豬，」愛麗絲回答，「希望你不要老是這樣突然一會兒出現，一會兒又消失，把人搞得頭都暈了。」

「好的，」貓答應。這次牠消失得非常慢，開始是尾巴，最後是那張咧著嘴的笑臉，那個笑臉在身體消失後好久，還停留了好一會兒。

「哎呀！我常常看見沒有笑臉的貓，」愛麗絲想，「可是還從沒見過沒有貓的笑臉呢！這真是我見過最奇怪的事了。」

她沒走多遠，就看見三月兔的房子了。她猜想這一定是三月兔的房子了，因為煙囪像長長的耳朵，屋頂還舖著兔子毛。房子很大，所以她先咬了口左手的蘑菇，讓自己長到六十公分高，才膽怯地走近，一邊對自己說：「要是牠瘋得很厲害，該怎麼辦才好？我還倒不如去找帽匠！」

想一想

當愛麗絲說：「去哪裡我都不太在乎」時，你覺得為什麼柴郡貓會回答：

「那你走哪條路都沒關係」呢？

第七章　瘋狂茶會

屋前有一棵大樹，樹下放著一張桌子。三月兔和帽匠坐在桌旁喝茶，一隻睡鼠在他們中間睡得正香，那兩個傢伙拿牠當墊子，將手臂支在睡鼠身上，而且就在牠的頭上交談著。「這隻睡鼠一定很難受，」愛麗絲想，「不過牠睡著了，可能不太在乎了。」

桌子很大，但他們三個卻都擠在桌子的一角，「沒位置啦！沒位置啦！」一看到愛麗絲走過來，他們就大聲嚷嚷。「明明就還有很多位置！」愛麗絲很不高興地說，一邊在桌子一端的大扶手椅上坐下來。

「要喝點酒嗎？」三月兔殷勤地問。

愛麗絲看了桌上一眼，除了茶什麼也沒有。「我沒看到酒啊！」她回答。

「本來就沒有酒啊！」三月兔說。

「那你說要請我喝酒就不太禮貌了。」愛麗絲氣憤地說。

「沒有人邀請你就坐下來，那也不太有禮貌。」三月兔回敬她一句。

「我不知道這是你的桌子，」愛麗絲說：「再說這裡可以坐得下很多人啊，不止三個！」

「你的頭髮該剪了。」帽匠說，他好奇地看了愛麗絲一會兒，這是他第一次開口。

「你不應該隨便評論別人，」愛麗絲板著臉說：「這樣有失禮貌。」

帽匠聽了之後瞪大了眼睛，但他只說了一句：「為什麼烏鴉會像一張寫字台呢？」

「好了，這下我們可有好玩的了！」愛麗絲想，「很高興他們給我謎語猜。」她大聲說：「我一定能猜出來。」

「你的意思是你能找到答案嗎？」三月兔問。

「沒錯，正是這樣。」愛麗絲說。

「那你怎麼想就怎麼說。」三月兔繼續說。

「我一直都這樣做的，」愛麗絲急忙回答：「至少……至少凡是我所說的就是我所想的——這是同一回事，你知道的。」

「根本不是同一回事，」帽匠說：「你能說『凡是我吃的東西我都能看見』和『凡是我看見的東西我都能吃』也算是同一回事嗎？」

「你能說，」三月兔也加了進來，「『是我的東西我都喜歡』和『我喜歡的東西都是我的』是同一回事嗎？」

「你能說，」睡鼠也像在說夢話一樣加入他們：「你能說『我睡覺時總在呼吸』和『我呼吸時總在睡覺』也是同一回事嗎？」

「對你而言倒真是一樣的，」帽匠答了一句。說到這裡，大家的談話中斷了，沉默了一會兒，愛麗絲費力地想著有關烏鴉和寫字台的事，可是她知道的實在不多。

過了不久，還是帽匠先開口：「今天是這個月的幾號？」他一面轉身問愛麗絲，一面從衣袋裡掏出一隻懷錶，不安地看著，還不停地搖晃，拿到耳朵旁聽聽。

愛麗絲想了一想回答：「四號。」

「錯了兩天！」帽匠嘆了口氣說，然後又生氣地看著三月兔說了一句：

「我告訴過你不應該用奶油塗錶的零件的。」

「這是最好的奶油了！」三月兔辯白說。

「沒錯，可是你一定把那些麵包屑也弄了進去，」帽匠抱怨，「你不應該用麵包刀挖奶油。」

三月兔很沮喪地拿起懷錶看了看，然後把它放到茶杯裡泡了一會兒，又拿出來看了看，可是除了一開始說的那句「這是最好的奶油了」，再也說不出別的了。

愛麗絲好奇地從他肩膀上看過去。「多麼好玩的手錶啊，」她說：「只報

日期，卻不報時間。

「為什麼一定要報時間呢？」帽匠嘀咕，「難道你的錶能告訴你年份嗎？」

「當然不能，」愛麗絲隨口答道：「但那是因為一年要很久才會過去。」

「我的錶不報時間也是這個原因。」帽匠說。

愛麗絲覺得實在莫名其妙，帽匠的話聽起來似乎毫無意義，但他說的的確是中文沒錯。「我不太懂你的意思。」她很有禮貌地說。

「睡鼠又睡著了，」帽匠說，隨後在睡鼠的鼻子上倒了點熱茶。

睡鼠不耐煩地晃了晃頭，眼睛睜都不睜就說：「就是，就是，我自己正要這麼說呢！」

「你猜到那個謎語了嗎？」帽匠對愛麗絲說。

「沒有，我放棄，」愛麗絲回答：「謎底到底是什麼？」

「我也不知道。」帽匠說。

「我也是。」三月兔說。

愛麗絲輕輕嘆了一口氣說：「我想你應該要珍惜點時間，像這樣出個沒有謎底的謎語，簡直是白白浪費時間。」

「如果你也像我一樣了解時間，」帽匠說：「你就不會叫它『時間』，而會稱呼它為『老兄』。」

「我不懂你說的是什麼意思。」愛麗絲說。

「你當然不懂，」帽匠得意地晃著頭說：「我敢說，你從來沒有和時間說過話。」

「應該沒有，」愛麗絲小心翼翼地回答說：「可是我在學音樂的時候，知道要按照時間打拍子的。」

「啊，你看吧！」帽匠說：「像你那樣拍打他，他會高興嗎？要是你和他交情好一點，他會叫時鐘聽你的話，譬如說，早上九點鐘要上課了，但你只要悄悄地暗示時間一聲，時鐘就會唰地轉到一點半，吃飯時間到了！」

「我真巴不得現在就是吃飯的時間。」三月兔小聲地自言自語說。

「那真是太棒了！」愛麗絲沉思著說：「可是，要是我肚子還不餓該怎麼辦呢？」

「剛開始也許還不餓，」帽匠說：「但是只要你喜歡，你可以叫時鐘一直固定在一點半，想停多久都可以。」

「你就是這麼做的嗎？」愛麗絲問道。

「我現在不行了，」他回答：「我和時間在三月份吵了一架——就是他發瘋之前。」他用茶匙指著三月兔，「那是在紅心皇后舉行

的一次盛大的音樂會上，我唱了一首：

滿天都是小蝙蝠！

一閃一閃亮晶晶！

你應該有聽過這首歌吧？」

「我聽過類似的。」愛麗絲說。

「接著，你聽，」帽匠繼續說：「接下來幾句是這樣唱的：

好像許多小茶盤，

掛在天空放光明。

一閃一閃——」

這時，睡鼠抖了抖身體，在睡夢中唱道：「一閃，一閃，一閃——」唱個不停，直到他們擰了牠一下才停止。

「我還沒唱完第一段，」帽匠說：「皇后就突然站起來大吼：『他在謀殺時間，砍掉他的頭！』」

「多麼野蠻殘忍呀！」愛麗絲驚喊起來。

帽匠傷心地接著說：「自從那次之後，不管我求他什麼他都不肯再滿足我的要求了，所以現在總是停在六點鐘。」

這時愛麗絲的腦子裡突然閃過一個聰明的念頭，於是她問道：「所以這就是這裡有這麼多茶具的原因，對嗎？」

「是的，就是這個原因，」帽匠嘆了口氣說：「永遠都停留在喝茶的時間，根本沒有空去洗茶具。」

「所以你們就圍著桌子移動位置，是不是？」愛麗絲問。

「沒錯，」帽匠說，「茶具用髒了，我們就往下個位置挪。」

「可是你們繞回原點之後怎麼辦呢？」愛麗絲追著問。

「我們換個話題好不好，」三月兔打著呵欠插嘴說道：「這個話題我已經聽煩了。我提議讓小女孩給我們講個故事吧！」

「我怕我一個故事都不會講！」愛麗絲說，她對這個提議感到非常慌亂。

「那就讓睡鼠講一個！」三月兔和帽匠一齊喊道，「醒一醒，睡鼠！」說著他們便從兩邊一起擰牠。

睡鼠慢慢睜開眼睛，嘶啞著嗓子說：「我又沒睡著，你們說的每一個字我都在聽呢。」

「給我們講個故事！」三月兔說。

「是啊，請講一個吧！」愛麗絲懇求道。

「快點講，要不然你又睡著了。」帽匠加上一句。

「從前有三個小姊妹，」睡鼠急急忙忙地講了起來，「她們的名字是，埃爾西、萊斯和蒂爾莉，她們住在一口井底下……」

「她們吃什麼過活呢？」愛麗絲對吃喝問題總是表現出濃厚的興趣。

「她們吃糖漿。」睡鼠想了一、兩分鐘說道。

「這怎麼行呢？總是吃糖漿，她們會生病的。」愛麗絲輕聲地說。

「就是因為這樣，她們都生病了，而且病得非常厲害。」睡鼠說。

愛麗絲努力地想像這樣特別的生活方式會是什麼樣子，可是怎麼想都想不出來。於是，她又接著問：「她們為什麼要住在井底下呢？」

「再多喝一點茶吧！」三月兔誠懇地對愛麗絲說。

「我連一點都還沒喝到呢！怎麼能說再多喝一點呢？」愛麗絲頗不高興地回答。

「你應該說你不能再少喝了，」帽匠說：「比沒有喝再多喝一點是最容易不過的了。」

「又沒人問你，」愛麗絲說。

「你剛才說我很失禮，那現在又是誰失禮了呢？」帽匠得意洋洋地說。

這回愛麗絲真是無言以對了，只得自己倒了點茶，拿了點奶油麵包，然後轉向睡鼠，重複了一遍自己的問題：「她們為什麼要住在井底下呢？」

睡鼠又想了一、兩分鐘後說：「因為那是一個糖漿井。」

「糖漿井，絕對沒有這樣的井！」愛麗絲認真起來。這時帽匠和三月兔發出「噓！噓！」的聲音，睡鼠也惱怒地說：「要是你再這樣不禮貌，那麼你最好自己來把故事講完！」

「不，請你繼續說下去吧！」愛麗絲低聲懇求說：「我再也不打岔了，我想也許有那樣的一個井吧！」

「當然有啊！」睡鼠煞有其事地說，然後又繼續往下講：「這三個小姊妹學著去抽——」

「抽什麼啊？」愛麗絲忘了自己的承諾，又開口問了。

「糖漿。」睡鼠這次毫不遲疑地回答。

「我想要個乾淨的茶杯，」帽匠插嘴說：「我們全都挪動一下位置吧！」

說著他就挪到下一個位置，睡鼠緊隨其後，三月兔跟著移到了睡鼠的位置上，愛麗絲也只好很不情願地坐到三月兔的位置上。這次挪動唯一得到好處的是帽匠，而愛麗絲的位置卻比以前差多了，因為三月兔剛才把牛奶瓶打翻在他的盤子上。

愛麗絲不想再得罪睡鼠，所以非常謹慎地問道：「不過我還是不懂，她們是從哪裡把糖漿取出來的呢？」

「你能夠從水井裡汲水，」帽匠說：「所以你也應該能從糖漿井裡汲取糖漿，對不對，笨蛋？」

「可是她們自己在井裡呀！」愛麗絲對睡鼠說，根本沒有理會帽匠說的最後一句話。

「當然她們是在井裡啦，」睡鼠說，「而且還在很裡面呢！」

這個回答完全把可憐的愛麗絲弄糊塗了，以致於她讓睡鼠一直講下去，沒有打斷牠。

「她們學著怎麼汲取東西，」睡鼠接著說，一邊打了個呵欠，又揉揉眼睛，牠已經非常睏了，「她們什麼東西都汲取，只要是『ㄇ』開頭的。」

「為什麼是『ㄇ』開頭的？」愛麗絲問。

「為什麼不行？」三月兔說。

愛麗絲沒有說話。這時，睡鼠已經閉上眼睛開始打盹，但是被帽匠擰了一下，尖叫一聲又醒過來，於是接著講下去：「『ㄇ』開頭的東西，例如貓咪、夢境，還有滿滿的。我們常說『滿滿的』，你知道滿滿的兔子是什麼嗎？」

「你問我嗎？」這下把愛麗絲難倒了，她說：「我還沒想⋯⋯」

「既然還沒想，你就不該說話！」帽匠說。

這句粗暴無禮的話讓愛麗絲再也無法忍受，於是她憤憤地站起來轉身就走，睡鼠也立刻睡著了。而那兩個傢伙一點也不在意愛麗絲是不是走掉了。她還回頭看了一、兩次，希望他們能夠挽留自己。當她最後一次回頭看他們時，他們正在想辦法把睡鼠塞進茶壺裡去。

「不管怎麼樣我都不會再去那裡了，」愛麗絲一邊在樹林中找路，一邊說：「這是我這輩子見過最愚蠢的茶會了。」

就在她嘀嘀咕咕的同時，她注意到有顆樹上有一扇門開著，可以通往樹林裡。「這可真奇怪！」她想，「不過今天的每件事都很奇怪，乾脆進去看看吧！」於是她走了進去。

她發現自己又再一次來到那個長長的大廳裡了，就站在那個小玻璃桌子旁邊。「哈，這次我可不能搞砸了！」說完她就拿起那把小金鑰匙，打開花園的門，然後輕輕地咬了一口蘑菇（她還留了一小塊在口袋裡），直到自己變成大約三十公分高，然後走過那條小走廊。接下來，她發現自己終於進入那個美麗的花園，走在漂亮的花圃和清涼的噴泉之中了。

如果你也可以像帽匠那樣要求時間停在你想要的地方，那你會希望時間停在什麼時候？為什麼？

第八章 皇后的槌球場

靠近花園的入口有一棵大玫瑰樹,樹上的花是白色的,但卻有三個園丁忙著把白花染紅。愛麗絲覺得這太奇怪了,走過去想看看。當她走近他們時,聽見其中一個對另一個說:「小心點,黑桃五!別把顏料濺了我一身。」

「我也沒有辦法啊,」黑桃五顯得有些不高興,「是黑桃七碰到了我的手臂啊。」

聽到這句話,黑桃七抬起頭說:「對啦,對啦,黑桃五!全部都是別人的錯啦!」

「你最好閉上嘴巴,」黑桃五說:「昨天我聽到皇后說,你的頭應該被砍下來!」

「爲什麼啊？」第一個說話的聲音問道。

「這不關你的事，黑桃二！」黑桃七說。

「不，當然跟他有關！」黑桃五說：「我來告訴他——是因爲你錯把鬱金香根當成洋蔥拿給了廚師！」

黑桃七把手上的刷子往下一扔說：

「好吧，在所有不公平的事情當中——」他突然看到了愛麗絲，愛麗絲正站在那裡注視著他們。於是他馬上住口，其他人也回過頭來，然後他們都深深地鞠了一個躬。

「你們能不能告訴我，」愛麗絲好奇而膽怯地問道：「為什麼你們要染玫瑰花呢？」

黑桃五和黑桃七都默不吭聲，看著黑桃二。黑桃二低聲地說：「其實是因為，小姐，你看，這裡應該種紅玫瑰的，結果我們錯種成白玫瑰，要是被皇后發現，我們全都得被砍頭。所以，小姐你看，我們正在盡最大的努力，想在皇后駕臨前，把……」就在此時，一直焦慮不安四處張望的黑桃五突然喊道：

「皇后！皇后！」這三個園丁立刻臉朝地趴了下來。

一陣腳步聲傳了過來，愛麗絲東張西望，希望能看見皇后。

最先走來的是十個手拿狼牙棒的士兵，他們全和那三個園丁一模一樣，長得像長方形的平板，手和腳長在板的四角上。後面跟著十名侍臣，他們渾身都是方塊，像那些士兵一樣，兩個兩個並排行進。侍臣的後面是王室的孩子們，有十幾個，一對對手拉著手，蹦蹦跳跳，興高采烈地跑過來，他們全部都裝飾著紅心。後面走來的是賓客，大多數賓客也都是國王和皇后。在那些賓客中，

愛麗絲認出了那隻白兔，牠正說著話，一副慌忙且神經質的樣子，別人對牠說話時，牠都點頭微笑，走過時並沒注意到愛麗絲。接著，就是個紅心傑克，雙手捧著放在紫紅色天鵝絨墊子上的王冠。這龐大隊伍的最後，才是紅心國王和皇后。

愛麗絲不知道該不該像那三個園丁那樣，臉朝地趴下，她根本不記得王室行列經過時，還有這麼一條規矩。「再說，」她心裡想著，「如果人們都臉朝下趴著，完全看不到列隊，那還有什麼意義呢？」於是她一動也不動地站在那裡等著。

隊伍走到愛麗絲面前時，全都停下來看著她。皇后威嚴地問：「這是誰？」這話是對紅心傑克說的，可是他只以鞠躬和微笑回應。

「白癡！」皇后不耐煩地搖搖頭說，然後轉向愛麗絲，「你叫什麼名字，孩子？」

「我叫愛麗絲，陛下。」愛麗絲非常有禮貌地回答，但是她又接著對自己

補上一句：「為什麼，他們只不過是一副撲克牌。我用不著怕他們！」

「這幾個又是誰？」皇后指著那三個趴在玫瑰樹旁邊的園丁。他們圍著一棵樹趴著，背上的圖案和其他撲克牌一樣，根本分不出他們是園丁、士兵、侍臣，還是她自己的三個孩子。

「我怎麼會知道？」愛麗絲回答，對自己的勇氣也感到很驚奇，「這又不關我的事。」

皇后的臉一下子氣得通紅，雙眼像野獸一樣瞪了愛麗絲許久，然後尖聲叫道：「砍掉她的頭！砍掉──」

「胡說八道！」愛麗絲鎮定且大聲地說。皇后就不作聲了。

國王用手拉了一下皇后的手臂，小聲地說：「冷靜點，親愛的，她不過是個孩子！」

皇后生氣地從國王身邊走開了，並對傑克說：「把他們翻過來！」

傑克小心翼翼地用腳把他們三個翻過來。

「起來！」皇后尖聲叫道。那三個園丁趕緊爬起來，開始向國王、皇后、王室的孩子們以及其他人鞠躬。

「好了，給我停下來！」

皇后尖叫：「把我的頭都給弄暈了！」她轉身朝著玫瑰樹的方向繼續說：「你們在這裡幹什麼？」

「陛下，願您開恩，」黑桃二單腳跪地，語氣十分謙

恭，「我們正想……」

「我知道了！砍掉他們的頭！」皇后仔細看了那些玫瑰花之後說。隊伍又繼續前進，只留下三個士兵行刑。三個倒楣的園丁急忙跑向愛麗絲，請求她的保護。

「你們不會被砍頭的！」愛麗絲邊說，邊把他們藏進旁邊的大花盆裡。三個士兵四處尋找，找了幾分鐘依然沒有找到，只好悄悄趕去追上自己的隊伍。

「把他們的頭砍掉了嗎？」皇后怒吼道。

「他們的頭已經砍掉了，陛下！」士兵高聲回答。

「好極了！」皇后說：「你會玩槌球嗎？」

「會！」愛麗絲大聲回答。

「那麼你過來！」皇后又吼道。於是愛麗絲也加入隊伍之中，她心裡盤算著以後會發生什麼事呢？

「今天……今天天氣真好呵！」愛麗絲聽到身旁一個怯怯的聲音在說話。

原來她正巧走在白兔的旁邊，而白兔正惴惴不安地偷看她的臉色。

「好天氣！」愛麗絲說：「公爵夫人呢？」

「噓！噓！」兔子急忙低聲制止她，並且擔心地轉過頭向皇后看看，然後踮起腳尖，把嘴湊到愛麗絲的耳邊悄悄地說：「她被判了死刑。」

「為什麼？」愛麗絲問。

「你是說真可憐嗎？」兔子問。

「不，不是，」愛麗絲回答說：「我沒想到可憐不可憐的問題，我是在問為什麼？」

「她打了皇后一個耳光……」兔子

說。愛麗絲笑出聲來了。「噓！」兔子害怕地低聲說：「皇后會聽到的！你知道，公爵夫人來晚了，皇后就說……」

「各就各位！」皇后雷鳴般地喊了一聲，他們就東竄西跑地找地方，撞來撞去的，一、兩分鐘後總算站好位置，比賽開始了。

愛麗絲覺得自己一輩子都沒見過這樣奇怪的槌球比賽。球場上到處都凹凸不平，槌球是活生生的刺蝟，槌球棒是用活生生的紅鶴，而士兵們則手腳著地當球門。

愛麗絲覺得最困難的是操縱紅鶴，

不過後來總算成功把紅鶴的身體穩穩地夾在手臂下，讓牠的腿垂著。可是，當她好不容易把紅鶴的脖子弄直，準備用牠的頭去打刺蝟時，紅鶴卻把脖子扭上來，用奇怪的表情看著愛麗絲，惹得愛麗絲大笑起來。她只得再把紅鶴的頭按下去，當她準備再一次打球的時候，卻惱火地發現刺蝟已經爬走了。除此之外，愛麗絲發現把刺蝟球打過去的路上總有一些小隆起或溝壑，而且躬起腰做球門的士兵常常站起來走到球場其他地方去。愛麗絲不久就得出一個結論：

這真是一個非常困難的遊戲。

那些打球的人也不按照次序，大家同時亂打，不是互罵，就是為了搶刺蝟而打起架來。沒多久，皇后大發雷霆，跺著腳走來走去，大喊：「砍掉他的頭！」或「砍掉她的頭！」幾乎每一分鐘就喊一次。

愛麗絲也十分擔心，雖然到目前為止，她還沒有和皇后發生爭吵，可是她知道隨時可能都會發生。「如果真的和皇后吵架的話，」她心想：「我會怎麼樣呢？這裡的人太喜歡砍別人的頭了！可是很奇怪，到現在都還有人活著。」

於是，愛麗絲想找一條能逃走的路，她思索著該如何在脫身時不被人發現。這時，她注意到天空出現一個奇怪的影子。剛開始她驚奇極了，看了一、兩分鐘後，才發現那是一個笑臉，於是她對自己說：「那是柴郡貓，現在終於有人可以和我說話了。」

「你好嗎？」當柴郡貓一露出能說話的嘴愛麗絲就問牠。

愛麗絲一直等到牠的眼睛出現才行，至少出來一隻再說話。「現在跟牠說話沒有用，」她想，「要等到牠的兩隻耳朵也出現了，愛麗絲才放下紅鶴，對牠說起這場槌球比賽的情況。能有個聽眾讓她非常高興。那隻貓似乎認為露出的部分已經夠了，就沒有再顯露出整個身體。

「我覺得他們這種玩法一點都不公平，」愛麗絲抱怨地說：「他們老是吵架，連自己說的話都聽不清楚了──而且他們好像沒有一定的規則，就算有，恐怕也沒人遵守──還有，你簡直無法想像，每一樣東西都是活的，真麻煩！

譬如說，我馬上就要把球打進球門了，但那個球門卻開始散起步來；當我正準備用自己的球擊皇后的刺蝟球時，牠一看到我的球拔腿就跑掉啦！」

「你喜歡皇后嗎？」貓低聲問道。

「一點都不喜歡，」愛麗絲說：「她非常——」剛說到這裡，她忽然發覺皇后就在她身後聽著，於是馬上改口說：「——非常會玩球，感覺不管再怎麼樣她都會贏的，所以我覺得根本不該再繼續玩下去。」

皇后微笑著走開了。

「你在跟誰說話？」國王走到愛麗絲面前，非常好奇地看著那個貓頭。

「請允許我介紹一下，這是我的朋友——柴郡貓。」愛麗絲說。

「我一點也不喜歡牠的樣子，」國王說：「不過，要是牠願意，可以吻我的手背。」

「我可不願意。」貓回答。

「不得無禮！」國王說：「而且別這樣看著我！」他邊說邊躲到愛麗絲的

身後。

「貓是可以看國王的，我在哪本書上讀過這句話，不過不記得是哪本書了。」愛麗絲說。

「喂，得把這隻貓弄走！」國王堅決地說，他叫住正好經過的皇后，「親愛的，希望你能把這隻貓弄走。」

皇后解決大小問題的辦法只有一個。「砍掉牠的頭！」她看也沒看就說。

「我親自去找劊子手。」國王很殷勤地說著，匆匆忙忙地走了。

愛麗絲⋯⋯還是回去看看遊戲進行得怎麼樣好了。她聽到皇后在遠處尖聲吼著──她已經聽到皇后宣判了三名錯過自己場次的球員死刑了。愛麗絲一點都不喜歡這個場面，整個比賽亂糟糟的，她根本不知道什麼時候輪到自己。於是她就去找她的刺蝟球。

她的刺蝟正在和另一隻刺蝟打架，愛麗絲看出這是一個用刺蝟球打中另一個刺蝟球的好機會，可是她的紅鶴跑到花園的另一邊去了，正想往樹上飛，卻

又飛不上去。

等她把紅鶴抓回來，那兩隻刺蝟已經跑得無影無蹤了。愛麗絲想：「其實這也沒什麼關係，反正這邊的球門都跑了，就算我現在有球也沒有用。」為了不讓紅鶴逃跑，愛麗絲把牠夾在手臂下，然後回到朋友那裡聊天去了。

愛麗絲回到柴郡貓那裡時，驚訝地發現有一大群人圍著牠，劊子手、國王、皇后正在激烈地辯論著。他們同時說著話，其他人都默不作聲，看起來十分不安。

愛麗絲一出現，三人就立即請她當公證人解決問題，他們爭先恐後地同時向她重複自己的理由，使得愛麗絲很難聽清楚他們在說什麼。

劊子手的理由是：除非有身體，不然就沒辦法砍頭，他說他從來沒做過這種事，而且這輩子他也不打算做這樣的事。

國王的理由是：只要有頭，就能砍，劊子手只要行刑就行了，哪來那麼多廢話。

皇后的理由是：要是不立刻執行她的命令，她就要把每個人的頭都砍掉（正是她最後這句話，讓這些人嚇得要命）。

愛麗絲想不出辦法來，只好說：「貓是公爵夫人的，你們最好去問問她的意見。」

「她在監獄裡，」皇后對劊子手說：「把她帶過來！」劊子手像箭一樣飛快地跑去了。

他一離開，貓頭就開始消失，等劊子手帶著公爵夫人回來時，貓頭已經完全不見了。國王和劊子手發瘋似地跑來跑去到處找，而其他人又回去玩槌球比賽了。

你覺得為什麼皇后只要一生氣就大吼她要砍下別人的頭？

第九章 假海龜的故事

「你一定不知道再見到你我有多麼高興！親愛的老朋友！」公爵夫人邊說邊親切地挽著愛麗絲的手臂，一起往前走。

愛麗絲看到公爵夫人心情這麼好，非常高興，她想上次在廚房見面時，公爵夫人會那麼兇，也許是受了胡椒刺激的關係。

愛麗絲自言自語地說（雖然她的口氣並沒有很大的把握）：「要是我是公爵夫人，我絕對不讓廚房有一點胡椒

味。沒有胡椒，湯也一樣可以做得非常好喝——也許正是胡椒使得人們脾氣暴躁。」她對自己這個新發現十分興奮，於是就接著說：「是醋弄得人心酸溜溜的，而甘菊把人們弄得滿腹牢騷——只有吃了麥芽糖這類東西，孩子們才變得那麼乖巧。真希望人們懂得這些，那樣一來他們就不會吝於給孩子糖吃了。

你知道——」

愛麗絲想得如此出神，已經完全忘記了公爵夫人，因此聽到她在自己耳邊說話時，她倒吃了一驚。「親愛的，你在想心事嗎？想得都忘了聊天了。現在我還沒辦法告訴你這件事的教訓是什麼，不過等一會兒我就會想出來的。」

「或許其中沒什麼教訓。」愛麗絲大膽地發表意見。

「得了，得了，小孩子亂說，」公爵夫人說：「每件事都會引出經驗教訓的，只要你能夠發現。」她說話時，身體緊緊靠著愛麗絲。

愛麗絲不太喜歡靠她那麼近，因為首先，公爵夫人長得非常難看；其次，她的高度使得她的尖下巴正好擱在愛麗絲的肩膀上，弄得她的肩膀疼痛難忍。

然而，愛麗絲不想顯得太無禮，只好盡可能地忍耐。

「現在比賽進行得比較順利了。」愛麗絲沒話找話地說。

「是啊，」公爵夫人答道，「由此可見這件事的教訓是……『啊，是愛，愛是推動世界的力量啊！』」

「有人說，」愛麗絲小聲地說：「這是出於人們的自私自利。」

「喔，是啊！意思都一樣，」公爵夫人邊說，邊使勁地把尖下巴往愛麗絲的肩上壓了壓，「這個教訓是：『只要保持理智，說話就會謹慎。』」

「她真是喜歡從事情中尋找教訓啊！」愛麗絲想。

「我猜想你一定很奇怪我為什麼不摟你的腰，」停了一會兒後公爵夫人又說：「因為我跟你的紅鶴還不熟。讓我試一試行嗎？」

「牠會咬人的。」愛麗絲小心地回答，一點也不想讓她試。

「沒錯，」公爵夫人說：「紅鶴和芥末一樣，都會咬人的，這個教訓是……

『物以類聚。』」

「可是芥末不是鳥。」愛麗絲說。

「你可說到重點了。」公爵夫人說。

「我想那是一種礦物吧?」愛麗絲說。

「當然是啦!」公爵夫人說,她似乎對愛麗絲所說的每句話都表示贊同,「附近就有一個大芥末礦,這個教訓是:『我的東西越多,你的東西就越少。』」

「喔,我知道了!」愛麗絲大聲喊道,沒有注意到她最後一句話,「芥末是一種植物,樣子看起來不像,不過就是植物。」

「我非常同意你的看法,」公爵夫人說:「這裡面的教訓是:『你看像什麼就是什麼』……或者,你可以把話說得簡單一點……『永遠不要把自己想像成和別人心目中的你不一樣,因為你曾經、或可能曾經在人們心目中是另外一個樣子。』」

「如果能把您的話寫下來,我想我會比較容易理解,」愛麗絲很有禮貌地

說：「現在我有點跟不上你說的話。」

「這算得了什麼？要是我高興，還能說得更長。」公爵夫人得意地說。

「喔，您不用麻煩了。」愛麗絲說道。

「說什麼麻煩呢！」公爵夫人說：「剛才我說的每句話啊，都是送給你的禮物。」

「這樣的禮物可真省錢，」愛麗絲想，「幸虧別人不是這麼送生日禮物的。」不過她不敢大聲說出來。

「又在想什麼啦？」公爵夫人問道，說著又用她的尖下巴緊緊地頂了愛麗絲一下。

「我有思考的權利，」愛麗絲尖聲回答道，她覺得有點不耐煩了。

「沒錯，」公爵夫人說道：「正像豬有飛的權利一樣。這裡的教……」

愛麗絲大吃一驚，因為公爵夫人說到這裡聲音突然消失了，甚至連她最愛說的「教訓」也沒說完，挽著愛麗絲的那隻手臂也開始顫抖起來。愛麗絲抬頭

望去，發現皇后就站在她們面前，雙臂交叉，臉色陰沉得像暴風雨前的天色一樣。

「今天天氣真好，陛下。」公爵夫人低聲下氣地說。

「現在，我警告你！」皇后跺著腳嚷道，「要嘛滾開，要嘛把頭砍下來，你得立刻選擇一樣，馬上就選。」

公爵夫人選擇了離開，並且馬上就走掉了。

「我們繼續去玩槌球吧！」皇后對愛麗絲說。愛麗絲嚇得不敢吭聲，只得慢慢跟著她回到槌球場。

其他客人趁皇后不在，都跑到樹蔭下乘涼去了。他們一看到皇后回來，就

馬上又跑去玩槌球。皇后僅僅說了一句，誰要是耽誤一秒鐘，就要他們的命。

整個槌球比賽，皇后一刻不停地和別人爭吵，大聲嚷著：「砍掉他的頭！」、「砍掉她的頭！」那些被宣判死刑的人，立刻就被士兵帶去監禁起來，而那些執行命令的士兵也不能再回來做球門了。因此，過了約莫半個小時，球場上已經沒有任何一個球門了。除了國王、皇后和愛麗絲，所有參加槌球遊戲的人，都被判了死罪監禁起來。

這時，累得上氣不接下氣的皇后停了下來，對愛麗絲說道：「你看過假海龜嗎？」

「沒有，」愛麗絲說：「我連假海龜是什麼東西都不知道呢！」

「不是有假海龜湯嗎？」皇后說：「當然就有假海龜了。」

「我從來沒見過，也沒聽說過這種東西。」愛麗絲說。

「那麼就跟我來吧！」皇后說：「牠會講牠的故事給你聽的。」

當她們一起離開的時候，愛麗絲聽到國王小聲地對大家說：「你們都被赦

免了。」愛麗絲心想：「這倒是件好事。」皇后下令處死那麼多人，讓她心裡很難過。

過了不久，她們碰見一隻獅鷲，正在曬太陽睡覺（要是你不知道什麼是獅鷲，請看圖。）

「起來，懶東西！」皇后說：「帶這位小姐去看假海龜，聽牠講故事。我得回去檢查執行死刑的情況。」說完她就走了，留下愛麗絲獨自和獅鷲在一起。愛麗絲不大喜歡這個傢伙的模樣，但是比起來，與其和那個野蠻的皇后在一起，還不如跟牠在一起比較安全，所以，她就留下來等著。

獅鷲坐起來揉揉眼睛，看著皇后，直到她走得看不見了，才笑了起來，一半對著自己，一半衝著愛麗絲。

「你在笑什麼？」愛麗絲問道。

「她呀，」獅鷲說：「這全是她的想像，事實上，他們從來沒有砍過別人的頭。我們走吧！」

愛麗絲跟在他後面走，心想：「這裡不管誰都對我說『走吧』、『走吧』，我從來沒有被人這麼使喚來使喚去的。從來沒有！」

走了不久，他們遠遠就看見了那隻假海龜，正孤獨而悲傷地坐在一塊小岩石上。再走近一點，愛麗絲聽見牠的嘆息聲，好像牠的心都要碎了，她打從心底同情牠。

「什麼事讓牠如此傷心呢？」她這樣問獅鷲。而獅鷲的回答和剛才差不多……「這全是牠的想像，事實上，牠根本沒有什麼傷心事。走吧！」

他們走到假海龜面前，牠用一雙飽含著眼淚的大眼睛望著他們，一句話也不說。

「這位年輕的小姐想了解一下你的經歷，」獅鷲對假海龜說：「她是真的想知道。」

「我來告訴她，」假海龜語調深沉沉地說：「你們兩個都坐下，在我講完之前都別出聲。」

於是他們坐了下來。有幾分鐘誰都不說話。愛麗絲心裡暗想：「要是牠不起個頭，怎麼能講完？」但是她還是很耐心地等待著。

「從前從前，」假海龜深深地嘆了口氣，終於開口了……「我曾經是隻真正的海龜。」

這句話之後，又是一段長時間的沉默，只有獅鷲偶爾叫一聲……「啊，哈！」以及假海龜不斷發出的沉重抽泣聲。愛麗絲幾乎都想站起來說：「謝謝你，先生，謝謝你講的有趣故事。」但是，她覺得應該還有下文，所以仍然一聲不吭靜靜地坐著。

等了一會兒，假海龜終於又開口了，牠平靜了許多，只不過依然不時地抽泣一聲，「我們小的時候，都到海裡去上學。校長是一隻老海龜……我們都叫牠陸龜。」

「既然牠不是陸龜，爲什麼要這樣叫牠呢？」愛麗絲問。

「我們叫牠陸龜，因爲牠幫我們上課呀！」假海龜生氣地說：「你怎麼這麼笨啊！」

「這麼簡單的問題還要問，你眞該爲自己感到難爲情！」獅鷲說。說著兩人就靜靜地坐在那裡看著可憐的愛麗絲，看得她眞想找個地洞鑽進去。最後，獅鷲對假海龜說：「說下去，老兄，別介意。」

「是的，我們到海裡去上學，雖然你也許不相信……」

「我又沒說我不相信。」愛麗絲插嘴說。

「你說過！」假海龜說。

愛麗絲還沒來得及辯解，獅鷲就出聲：「住口！」然後假海龜又接著講下去……

「我們受的是最好的教育……事實上，我們每天都上學。」

「我也是天天都上學，」愛麗絲說：「這沒有什麼值得驕傲的。」

「你們也有選修課嗎？」假海龜有點不安地問道。

「當然啦，」愛麗絲說：「我們學法文和音樂。」

「也有洗衣課嗎？」假海龜問道。

「當然沒有。」愛麗絲生氣地回答。

「喔，那就不能算是一所真正的好學校，」假海龜鬆了一口氣，「我們學校的課程表最後一項都是選修課：法文、音樂、洗衣。」

「你們都住在海底，應該不用洗什麼衣服吧！」愛麗絲說。

「我實在無法上這種課，」假海龜嘆息了一聲說：「我只上正課。」

「都是學些什麼？」愛麗絲問道。

「一開始當然是蹣跚學步和蠕動了，」假海龜答道：「然後是學習各種運算方法──『夾法』、『鉗法』、『沉法』和『醜法』。」

「我從來沒聽說過『醜法』，」愛麗絲壯著膽子問：「那是什麼？」

獅鷲舉起了兩隻爪子驚訝地說：「什麼？你沒聽說過醜法？那我想你總該知道什麼叫美法吧！」

愛麗絲含糊地說：「是的，我知道，那是……讓什麼……東西……變得好看些的方法。」

「好，那麼，」獅鷲接著說：「如果你還是不知道什麼是醜法，一定是個傻瓜了。」

愛麗絲不敢再繼續談論這個問題了，於是她轉向假海龜問道：「你還學了些什麼？」

「我們還學歷史，」假海龜扳著手指頭說，「歷史有上古歷史、中古歷史和近代歷史，還要學地理和繪畫。我們的繪畫老師是一條老鰻魚，一星期來一次，教我們水彩畫和素描畫。」

「那是什麼樣子的呢？」愛麗絲問道。

「我沒辦法做給你看，我的身體太僵硬了，而獅鷲又從來沒學過這些。」假海龜說。

「那是因為我沒時間！」獅鷲說：「不過我聽過外語老師的課，牠是一隻

老螃蟹，是一隻真螃蟹。

「我從來沒有聽過牠的課，」假海龜嘆息著說：「人家說牠教的是臘丁和洗臘。」

「沒錯！就是這樣。」獅鷲也嘆了口氣，於是兩個傢伙都用爪子掩住了自己的臉。

「你們一天上多少課呢？」愛麗絲連忙換了個話題。

「第一天十小時，第二天九小時，依此類推。」假海龜回答。

「好奇怪的安排喔！」愛麗絲叫道。

「所以人們才說上『多少課』，」假海龜解釋說：「『多少課』就是先多後少的意思。」

第十一天就該放假了？」

對愛麗絲來說這可真是個新鮮的說法，她想了一會兒才接著說道：「那麼

「那當然啦！」假海龜說。

「那麼第十二天怎麼安排呢？」愛麗絲追問道。

「上課的問題談夠了，」獅鷲口氣堅決地插嘴說：「告訴她一些關於遊戲的事吧！」

你覺得為什麼這隻海龜會變成「假」海龜？

第十章 龍蝦方塊舞

假海龜深深地嘆了一口氣，用手背抹了抹眼淚。他望著愛麗絲想說話，可是有好一陣子泣不成聲。「牠好像嗓子裡卡了根骨頭。」獅鷲說，於是就搖晃了一下牠，再接著拍拍牠的背。後來假海龜終於開口說話了，牠一邊流著眼淚一邊說：「你大概沒在海底下長時間住過——」（「沒有住過，」愛麗絲說。）——「你大概從來沒見過龍蝦吧——」（愛麗絲剛想說「我吃過——」，但又立即忍住了，改口說「從來沒有」），「——所以你根本想像不出龍蝦方塊舞有多麼有趣！」

「是的，沒有辦法想像」愛麗絲說：「那是一種什麼樣的舞？」

獅鷲說：「大家先是在岸邊站成一排——」

「兩排！」假海龜嚷道：「有海豹、烏龜和鮭魚，統統排好隊。然後就把所有的水母都清理乾淨——」

「這可要費好一番工夫呢！」獅鷲插嘴說。

「然後，向前進兩步……」假海龜接著說。

「每個都有一隻龍蝦作舞伴！」獅鷲又嚷道。

「當然啦，」假海龜說道：「向前進兩步，找好舞伴……」

「再交換舞伴，向後退兩步。」獅鷲接著說。

假海龜說：「然後，就把龍蝦……」

「扔出去！」獅鷲跳起來嚷道。

「用盡全力把牠們遠遠地扔到海裡去。」

「再游過去把牠們追回來！」獅鷲尖聲叫道。

「接著在海裡翻一個肋斗！」假海龜邊叫邊發瘋似地跳來跳去。

「再交換一次舞伴！」獅鷲尖著嗓門嚷叫道。

「然後再回到陸地上，這就是舞蹈的第一節。」假海龜說著說著，音調突然降了下來。這兩個剛才像瘋子一般跳來跳去的傢伙，現在卻非常安靜而悲傷地坐下來，看著愛麗絲。

「那一定是很好看的舞蹈。」愛麗絲膽怯地說。

「你想看看嗎？」假海龜問。

「是的，很想看。」愛麗絲說。

「來，那我們來跳第一節吧！」假海龜對獅鷲說：「你看，就算沒有龍蝦，我們也能跳。不過誰來唱呢？」

「喔，你唱吧，」獅鷲說：「我已經忘記歌詞了。」

於是，他們相當嚴肅地圍著愛麗絲一本正經地跳起舞來，一面跳，一邊用前爪打著拍子。不時地跳到愛麗絲跟前，踩著愛麗絲的腳。假海龜緩慢而悲傷地唱著：

「鱈魚對蝸牛說：

『你不能走快一點嗎？

有一隻海豚正跟在我們後面，

他老是踩到我的尾巴。

你看龍蝦和烏龜多麼匆忙，

海灘舞會馬上就要開始了！

你願意去跳舞嗎？

你願去，你要去，

你願去，你要去，

你願去跳舞嗎？

你願去，你要去，

你願去，你要去，

你願去跳舞嗎？

你要去跳舞嗎？』

『你都不知道那有多好玩，我們和龍蝦一起被扔得老遠。」

『太遠了，太遠了！」蝸牛瞅了一眼回答。

他說謝謝鱈魚，

但他不願參加舞會。

他不能，他不能，他不願，他不願參加舞會。

他不願，他不能，他不願，他不能，

他不能參加舞會。

他的有鱗的朋友回答：

『扔得遠又有什麼關係？

在大海那邊，你知道的，

還有另一個海岸。

如果你離英國越遠，

就會越接近法國。

親愛的蝸牛，不要害怕，

趕快參加舞會。

你可願，你可要，你可要，

你可願參加舞會？

你可願，你可要，你可要，

你可願，你可要，

你可要參加舞會？』」

「謝謝你們，這舞真有趣，」愛麗絲說，她很高興舞蹈終於結束了，「尤

其是那首奇妙的關於鱈魚的歌真好玩。」

假海龜說：「喔，說到鱈魚，牠們……你應該見過牠們了吧？」

「是的，」愛麗絲回答，「在飯……」，她想說在飯桌上，但又覺得不安就急忙住嘴了。

「我不知道『飯』是什麼地方，」假海龜說：「不過，如果你經常看見牠們，當然就知道牠們長什麼樣子了。」

「我想是的，」愛麗絲邊想邊說：「牠們嘴裡咬著尾巴，身上還裹滿了麵包屑。」

「麵包屑？你一定是弄錯了！」假海龜說：「海水會把麵包屑沖掉的。不過牠們倒真會把尾巴彎到嘴裡，這是因為……」說著假海龜打一個呵欠，閉上眼睛。「告訴她是什麼原因。」他對獅鷲說。

獅鷲說：「這是因為牠們願意和龍蝦一起參加舞會，常常要被扔到海裡去，還要掉到很遠的地方，所以得緊緊咬住尾巴，結果尾巴從此就伸不直了。」

「謝謝你，」愛麗絲說：「真是很有意思，我以前從來不知道這麼多關於

鱈魚的故事。

「你要是願意，我還可以告訴你更多，」獅鷲說：「你知道牠們為什麼叫鱈魚嗎？」

「這我倒沒想過，」愛麗絲說：「為什麼呢？」

「因為牠是用來擦靴子和鞋子的。」獅鷲煞有其事地說。

愛麗絲被弄糊塗了。「擦靴子和鞋子？」她詫異地問。

「是的，你的鞋子是用什麼擦的？」獅鷲說：「我的意思是，用什麼把鞋子擦得那麼亮？」

愛麗絲低頭看了看自己的鞋子，想了一下才說：「我用的是鞋油。」

「海裡的靴子和鞋子，」獅鷲嗓音深沉地繼續說：「是用鱈魚的雪擦的。

現在你知道了。」

「那鱈魚的雪是用什麼做的？」愛麗絲好奇地追問。

「當然是鯧魚和鰻魚啦！」獅鷲顯得很不耐煩，「就算是小蝦子也會這樣

告訴你的。」

「如果我是鱈魚，」愛麗絲說，腦子裡還惦記著那首歌，「我會對海豚

說：『離我們遠一點，我們不想要你跟著我們！』」

「牠們不得不讓海豚跟著，」假海龜說：「聰明的魚不管到哪裡去都少不

了老海豚。」

「真的嗎？」愛麗絲驚奇地問。

「當然，」假海龜說：「如果有條魚前來告訴我牠準備要外出旅行，那麼

我就會說：『你準備帶哪條海豚去？』」

「你說什麼『孩童』？」愛麗絲問。

「我想說的就是我剛剛說的那些，」假海龜生氣地回答。獅鷲接著說：

「讓我們聽聽你的來歷吧！」

「要告訴你們我的故事——得從今天早晨開始，」愛麗絲有點膽怯地說：

「我們不必從昨天開始，因為從那以後，我已經變成另一個人了。」

「那你把來龍去脈解釋解釋。」假海龜說。

「不，不！先講你的經歷，再作解釋。」獅鷲等不及了，「長篇大論的解釋太浪費時間了。」

於是，愛麗絲開始講她的故事，她從看見那隻白兔開始說起。起初還有點緊張——那兩個傢伙坐得離她那麼近，一邊一個，眼睛和嘴巴又張得那麼大——但是到後來她的膽子逐漸大了起來。她的兩個聽眾一聲不響安靜地聽著，直到她講到背《你已經老了，威廉爸爸》給毛毛蟲聽，但背出來的字眼完全不對的時候，假海龜才長長嘆了一口氣，說道：「這真的很古怪。」

「怪得沒辦法再怪了。」獅鷲說。

「這首詩全背錯了！」假海龜若有所思地重複道，「我倒想再聽聽她背點什麼東西，讓她開始吧！」他看看獅鷲，好像他有權利能指使愛麗絲似的。

「站起來背《懶鬼的心聲》。」獅鷲對愛麗絲說。

「這些傢伙老是那麼喜歡支使人，還老愛要人背東西，」愛麗絲想，「我

還不如馬上回學校去呢！」然而，她還是站起身來開始背誦。不過她腦子裡滿是龍蝦方塊舞的事，簡直不知道自己在說些什麼。她背出來的東西聽起來確實非常奇怪：

「那是龍蝦的聲音，
我聽見他在說——
『你們把我烤得太黃，
我頭髮裡還得加點糖。』
他用自己的鼻子，
就像鴨子用自己的眼瞼一樣，
整理自己的腰帶和鈕釦，
還把腳趾向外扭轉。
當沙灘乾燥的時候，

他就像雲雀一樣快樂。

他洋洋得意地和鯊魚攀談，

但是當潮水上漲，鯊魚包圍住他，

他的聲音就變得膽怯而又抖顫！」

「這和我小時候背的完全不一樣。」獅鷲說。

「我以前也從來沒聽過，」假海龜說：「但這聽起來像是很不尋常的胡言亂語。」

愛麗絲什麼話也沒說，雙手摀著臉坐了下來，心裡想著不知道什麼時候才能恢復正常。

「我希望你把那首詩解釋一下。」假海龜說。

「她解釋不了，」獅鷲急忙說：「接著背下一節吧！」

「可是他的腳趾究竟是怎麼回事？」假海龜堅持問道：「他怎麼能用鼻子

扭轉腳趾呢？」

「那是跳舞的第一個姿勢，」愛麗絲說。但她自己已經被這一切弄得莫名其妙，所以也希望能換一個話題。

「那你來背背第二節吧，」獅鷲不耐煩地說道：「一開頭是『我經過他的花園』。」

愛麗絲不敢違背牠的意思，雖然她明知道一切都會弄錯的。她用顫抖的聲音背誦道：

「我經過他的花園，
用一隻眼睛看見，
豹和貓頭鷹，
正在分享一塊水果塔。
豹分到了外皮、肉汁和肉餡，

貓頭鷹只分到了一個空盤。

水果塔吃完以後，

貓頭鷹請求豹讓牠把湯匙放進口袋，

豹發出一聲怒吼，

把刀子和叉子通通拿走。

宴會就此結束——」

「把全部的句子都背出來有什麼用？」假海龜插嘴打斷她，「還不如一邊背一邊解釋，這是我聽過最亂七八糟的東西了。」

「沒錯，最好停下來！」獅鷲說，這正是愛麗絲求之不得的事。

「那我們要再跳一節龍蝦方塊舞嗎？」獅鷲接著說：「不然，就請假海龜為你唱首歌吧！」

「喔，一首歌，我想聽，如果假海龜願意的話。」愛麗絲的語氣如此迫不

及待，惹得獅鷲有點不是滋味：「哼！毫無品味可言！老兄，你就唱那首『海龜湯』給她聽聽怎麼樣？」

假海龜深深地嘆了一口氣，哽咽著唱起來：

「美味的湯，裝在熱氣騰騰的碗裡。

綠色的濃湯，

誰不願意嚐一嚐，

這樣的好湯。

晚餐用的湯，美味的湯，

晚餐用的湯，美味的湯，

美——味的湯——湯！

美——味的湯——湯！

美——味的湯——湯！

晚——晚——晚餐用的——湯，

美味的，美味的湯！

美味的湯！

有了它，誰還會想著魚，

想著要吃野味和別的菜？

誰不想嚐一嚐，

一塊錢一碗的好湯？

一塊錢一碗的好湯？

美——味的湯——湯！

美——味的湯——湯！

晚——晚——晚餐用的湯……湯，

美味的，美——味的湯！」

「合唱部分再來一遍！」獅鷲喝采道。假海龜剛要開口，就聽到遠處傳來一聲高喊：「審判開始啦！」

「走吧！」獅鷲叫道，他拉著愛麗絲的手，不等那首歌唱完就急急忙忙跑走了。

「什麼審判呀？」愛麗絲一面跑一面喘著氣問，但是獅鷲只是說：「快點！」。他跑得更快了。他們的身後，微風送來越來越微弱的歌聲：

「晚——晚——晚餐用的湯——湯，

美味的，美味的湯！」

在看了假海龜和獅鷲的教學後，你會不會想要嘗試跟著跳「龍蝦方塊舞」？

第十一章　誰偷了水果塔？

當他們趕到法庭時，紅心國王和紅心皇后正坐在王座上，身邊圍著一大群各式各樣的小鳥和小獸，就像一整副撲克牌。紅心傑克站在他們面前，被鏈條鎖著，兩邊各有一名士兵看守。國王旁邊就是那隻白兔，一手拿著喇叭，一手拿著一卷羊皮紙文件。法庭正中央有一張桌子，上面放著一大盤水果塔。水果塔十分精緻，愛麗絲看一眼就覺得餓了。她想：「真希望審判能快一點結束，好讓大家吃點心。」但是，看來並沒有這種跡象。於是，她只好東張西望打發時間。

以前，愛麗絲從來沒有到過法庭，只曾經在書上看過。她因為自己幾乎知道這裡所有的事物而有些得意。「那位是法官，」她對自己說：「因為他戴著

不以『生物』來統稱，因為有的是動物，有的是鳥類）一定是陪審員了。」最後這一句，她對自己說了兩、三遍，覺得很引以為傲。因為在她看來，幾乎沒有像她這種年紀的女孩懂得這麼多。即使說「法律審查員」她們也不會懂的。

十二位陪審員全都在紙板上忙著寫東西。「牠們在那裡幹什麼？」愛麗絲低聲問獅鷲，「審判開始之前，他們應該沒有什麼要記錄的。」

獅鷲也低聲回答：「牠們在記自己的姓名，怕在審判結束前就忘掉。」

「假髮。」

這裡說明一下，那位法官就是國王。他在假髮上又戴了王冠，看起來很彆扭，而且肯定也不舒服。

「那是陪審團席，」愛麗絲想，「而那十二個生物（她不得

「真是笨東西！」愛麗絲不高興地大聲說，但立刻就住口，因為白兔正在高喊：「法庭肅靜。」這時，國王也戴上了眼鏡，迅速地掃視四周，想找出是誰在說話。

愛麗絲從那些陪審員背後偷偷看他們究竟在寫些什麼，結果發現所有的陪審員都在紙板上寫下了「笨東西」。有一個陪審員甚至不會寫「笨」，請求隔壁的生物告訴他。「我看還不到審判結束，牠們的紙板肯定就會寫得一塌糊塗了！」愛麗絲想。

一名陪審員的筆在書寫時發出刺耳的聲音，愛麗絲當然忍受不了，於是，她在法庭裡轉了一圈，走到牠背後，逮住機會一下子就把筆給抽走。她的動作非常迅速，那個可憐的小陪審員（就是那隻蜥蜴比爾）甚至還沒有弄清楚是怎麼回事。因此，在到處都找不到自己的鉛筆後，牠就只能用手指頭書寫了。當然這樣完全沒有用，因為手指在紙板上無法留下任何痕跡。

「傳令官，宣讀起訴書。」國王宣布說。

於是白兔吹了三下喇叭，然後打開羊皮紙上的文件，宣讀如下：

「紅心皇后，做了水果塔，

在一個炎炎的夏日；

紅心傑克，偷走了水果塔，

全都帶走匆匆遠離！」

「請陪審團裁決。」國王對陪審員說。

「不行，還不行！」兔子連忙插話道，「判決以前還有許多程序呢！」

於是，國王說：「傳喚第一個證人。」白兔吹了三聲喇叭，喊道：「傳第一位證人到庭！」

第一個證人就是那個帽匠。他進來時，一手拿著茶杯，另一隻手捏著一片

奶油麵包。他說：「請您原諒，陛下，我帶這些東西進來，是因為我還沒喝完茶就被傳喚來了。」

「你早就該喝完了，」國王說：「你是從什麼時候開始喝的？」

三月兔和睡鼠手挽著手也跟著他進來了，帽匠看著三月兔說：「我想是三月十四號開始的。」

「是十五號。」三月兔說。

「十六號。」睡鼠補充說。

「都記下來，」國王對陪審員說，陪審員連忙在紙板上寫下了三個日期，然後把它們加起來，再換算成新台幣。

「把帽子脫掉！」國王對帽匠說。

「帽子不是我的。」帽匠回答。

「偷來的！」國王大斥一聲，轉頭看了看陪審員。陪審員立刻記下「偷來的」，作為備忘錄。

「這是我留著賣的，我是帽匠，沒有一頂帽子是我自己的。」帽匠解釋。

這時，皇后戴上了眼鏡，開始盯著那帽匠，嚇得他臉色發白，侷促不安。

「拿出證據來，」國王說：「不要緊張，不然我就當場處決你。」

這番話不僅沒有為庭上的證人壯膽，反而使他更加不安地交替著雙腿，很緊張地看著皇后，而且由於心慌意亂，他竟然把茶杯當成奶油麵包咬了一大塊，很下來。

就在這時，愛麗絲有一種非常奇怪的感覺，剛開始她搞不清楚是怎麼一回事，過了一會兒才慢慢發現，她的身體又在長大了。起初，她還想站起來離開法庭，但隨即考慮了一下，決定要留下來，只要屋裡還有她容身的餘地。

「我希望你不要這樣子擠我，我都有點透不過氣來了。」坐在愛麗絲身邊的睡鼠說。

「沒有辦法啊，你看我還在長。」愛麗絲非常溫和地說。

「你沒有權利在這裡長。」睡鼠說。

「什麼啊，你自己也在長呀。」愛麗絲大膽地說。

「是沒錯，但是我長起來很有分寸，不是像你那種荒謬的長法。」睡鼠說著，不高興地站起來，走到法庭另一邊去。

就在愛麗絲和睡鼠說話的時候，皇后的眼睛一直沒有離開過帽匠。睡鼠走到法庭的另一邊時，她對一位官員說：「把上次音樂會上有唱歌的人的名單給我。」聽到這句話，可憐的帽匠嚇得全身發抖，甚至把兩隻鞋子都抖掉了。

「拿出證據，不然我就處死你，不管你是不是很緊張！」國王憤怒地重複了一遍。

「陛下，我只是個窮人，」帽匠聲音顫抖地說，「我只不過是才剛剛開始喝茶——還沒超過一星期——由於奶油麵包變得太薄——又由於茶會閃閃發亮——」

「什麼東西閃閃發亮？」國王問。

「我說茶。」帽匠回答。

「喔，擦，當然，擦火柴本來就會閃閃發亮。你以為我是笨蛋嗎？繼續說下去！」國王尖銳地吼道。

「我只是個窮人，」帽匠接著說：「從那以後，大部分的東西都會閃閃發亮——只有三月兔——」

三月兔趕緊插嘴：「我沒有說！」

「你有！」帽匠說。

「我否認！」三月兔說。

「既然牠不承認，那就略過這個部分吧。」國王說。

「好，那就是睡鼠說的——」說到這裡，帽匠四下張望，想知道睡鼠會不會否認，然而睡鼠什麼也沒說，他睡得正熟。

「從那以後，我多切了一些奶油麵包……」帽匠繼續說。

「但是睡鼠說了些什麼？」一位陪審員問。

「我不記得了。」帽匠說。

「你一定得記得，不然我就處決你。」國王說。

那個可憐的帽匠連忙丟掉茶杯和奶油麵包，單膝跪下說：「我是個可憐的窮人，陛下。」

「你是個可憐的狡辯者。」國王說。

這時一隻豚鼠突然喝起采來，但立即被法官制止了。（「制止」這個詞很令人費解，需詳細解釋一下才能明白是怎麼回事。他們用一個大帆布袋，把那隻豚鼠頭朝裡面塞了進去，用繩子綁住袋口，然後坐在袋子上。）

愛麗絲心想：「真高興能看到這件事。我常常在報紙上看到這樣的話，說審判結束時『出現了喝采聲，但立即被法官制止。』直到現在我才明白那是怎麼回事。」

「如果你知道的只有這麼多，那就退下去吧！」國王宣布。

「我實在無法再往下退了，因為我已經站在地板上了。」帽匠說。

「那你可以坐下。」國王說。

話才剛說完，又一隻豚鼠喝起采來，但隨即也被「制止」了。

愛麗絲心裡想：「好啦，那兩隻豚鼠都被收拾了！現在審判可以進行得順利一些了。」

「我還得喝完這杯茶。」帽匠說著，不安地看著皇后，皇后正在看唱歌的人的名單。

「你可以走了。」聽到國王這麼一說，帽匠連忙跑出法庭，根本顧不得穿上鞋子。

這時，皇后對一位官員吩咐了一句：「——現在去外面砍掉他的頭。」可是官員還沒有追到大門口，帽匠就跑得無影無蹤了。

「傳下一個證人！」國王吩咐。

下一個證人是公爵夫人的女廚師。她手裡拿著胡椒瓶，一走進法庭，就使得靠近她的人不停地打噴嚏，因此愛麗絲一下就猜出是誰了。

「說出你的證詞。」國王吩咐道。

「不要。」女廚師回答。

國王不安地看了看白兔，白兔低聲說：「陛下得盤問盤問這個證人。」

「好，如果非要這樣的話，我一定會這麼做的。」國王嘆了口氣說。他交叉雙臂，對女廚師皺著眉頭，一直皺到視線都模糊了，才用深沉的語調說：

「水果塔是用什麼做的？」

「大部分是用胡椒做的。」女廚師說。

「是用糖漿做的。」一個睏倦的聲音從女廚師身後傳來。

「掐住那隻睡鼠的脖子，」皇后尖叫起來：「砍掉他的頭，攆出法庭，制止他，掐死他，把他的鬍子拔光！」

整個法庭混亂了好幾分鐘，直到把睡鼠趕出去以後，大家才再次安靜地坐下來，但這時女廚師卻失蹤了。

「沒關係！」國王大大鬆了口氣，「傳下一個證人。」然後他對皇后耳語說：「說真的，親愛的，下一個證人一定得由你來審問了，我已經頭痛的無法忍受了。」

愛麗絲看到白兔正在整理名單，非常好奇，想看看下一位證人是誰。她想：「看來他們還沒有收集到足夠的證據。」但接著發生的事卻令她大吃一驚，白兔竟然用刺耳的嗓音喊道：「愛麗絲！」

想一想

當愛麗絲無法控制自己的身體長大時，為什麼睡鼠要指責她沒有權利在那裡長？

第十二章　愛麗絲的證詞

「在這裡！」愛麗絲喊道，她完全忘了自己在剛才的混亂時刻中已經長得很大了。她過於急促地站起來，使得裙擺掃過陪審團，把陪審員們打得四腳朝天，翻倒在下面聽眾的頭上，害得他們在人頭上爬來爬去，這讓愛麗絲想起一星期前她偶然打翻金魚缸的事。

「啊，實在是對不起！」愛麗絲驚慌失措地說，急急忙忙把那些陪審員扶回原位，因為金魚缸的事情還在她腦中盤旋，她隱約意識到，如果不立刻把陪審員放回席位上，他們會死去的。

「審判暫停！」國王嚴肅地宣布，「直到全體陪審員返回自己的位置。」

他狠狠地加重語氣，眼睛嚴厲地盯著愛麗絲。

愛麗絲看著陪審團席，發現由於自己的疏忽，竟然將蜥蜴頭朝下倒放著。那個可憐的小東西完全無法動彈，正著急地把尾巴擺來擺去。愛麗絲趕緊把牠拿起來擺正，不過她心想，「這樣做也不見得有什麼意義，不論頭朝哪邊，牠發揮的作用都差不多。」

等陪審員鎮定下來，紙板和鉛筆也都找到了以後，他們立即勤奮地工作起來。首先是記下剛才的偶發事故。除了蜥蜴以外，他已經精疲力盡，做不了任何事情，只能張著嘴坐著，兩眼無神地望著法庭的天花板。

國王開口了：「你知道這件事嗎？」

「不知道。」愛麗絲回答。

「什麼都不知道？」國王再問。

「什麼都不知道。」愛麗絲回答。

「這一點非常重要，」國王對陪審團說。就在陪審員把這些問答記在紙板上時，白兔忽然插嘴說：「陛下的意思是說當然是不重要的。」牠的語氣十分

恭敬，邊說邊對國王擠眉弄眼。

於是，國王連忙把話接過來：「當然，我本來說的就不重要。」——好像在試試看哪一個詞比較順口。

聲嘀咕道：「重要……不重要……重要……不重要……重要……」

有些陪審員記下了「重要」，有些記下了「不重要」。愛麗絲離陪審團很近，紙板上記的字她看得一清二楚，她心想：「其實不管他們怎麼寫，這些都沒關係。」

國王剛才忙著在記事本上記什麼東西，現在他又高聲喊道：「保持肅靜！」然後照著本子宣讀：「規則第四十二條，凡是身高超過一千五百公尺以上者退出法庭。」

所有人都望著愛麗絲。

「我不到一千五百公尺高。」愛麗絲說。

「你有。」國王說。

「將近三千公尺了。」皇后補充說。

「嗯，不管怎樣，我就是不走。」愛麗絲說：「再說，那根本不是正式的規定，是你剛才捏造出來的。」

「那可是書中最老的一條規定。」

「那就應該是第一條。」國王說。

國王臉色蒼白，急忙闔上本子，用顫抖且低沉的語調對陪審團說：「請陪審團做出裁決！」

「陛下！又發現新的證據了！」白兔急急忙忙跳起來說：「有人剛剛發現了這張紙。」

「上面寫著什麼？」皇后問。

「我還沒打開來呢！」白兔回答：「但看來像是一封信，是那個犯人寫給……給一個什麼人的。」

「毫無疑問的，肯定是這樣，」國王說：「除非它不是寫給任何人的，而

那樣可就不合情理了。」

「信是寫給誰的？」一個陪審員問。

「它不是寫給誰的，事實上，信封上什麼地址也沒寫。」白兔一面說，一面打開那張紙，然後又說：「啊！根本不是信，而是一首詩。」

「是犯人的筆跡嗎？」另一個陪審員問。

「不是，這太奇怪了。」白兔說，陪審員們全都露出迷惑不解的樣子。

「他一定是模仿別人的筆跡。」國王一說，陪審員們似乎又豁然了解了。

這時，傑克開口說：「陛下，這不是我寫的，誰也不能證明是我寫的，因為末尾並沒有簽名。」

「如果你沒有簽名，」國王說：「那只能說明你的罪行更惡劣。這意味著你的狡猾，否則你為什麼不像一個誠實的人那樣，簽上你的名字。」

這番話引起全場一片掌聲，這是那天國王所講出來的第一句聰明話。

「這就證明他有罪。」皇后說。

「這根本不能證明什麼！」愛麗絲說話了：「你們甚至連詩寫的是什麼都不知道！」

「快念一念！」國王命令道。

白兔戴上了眼鏡，問道：「我該從哪裡開始呢？陛下。」

「從起頭的地方開始，一直讀到末尾，然後停止。」國王鄭重地說。

白兔念的詩句如下：

他們告訴我，你去找過她，
又再向他提起我。
她說我人很好，
但說我不會游泳。

他對他們說我沒去，

（我們都知道這是真的）。

要是她不肯放手，

你想你會怎麼做？

我給她一，他們給他二，

你給我們三個或更多；

他們又從他那邊拿來還給你，

其實原本都是屬於我的。

要是我或她竟然也會

被這件事牽扯，

他拜託你放他們走，

就像我們曾做過的那樣。

我的看法是你早已是

（在她還沒說「呸」之前）

他和我們和它之間

一道難以橫越的障礙。

這是我們之間的祕密。

絕不能讓他人知道，

這件事必須永遠保密，

她最喜歡的是它們，

不要讓他知道

「這是到目前爲止我們所聽到最重要的證據了，」國王磨擦著雙手說：

「現在請陪審員──」

「如果有誰能解釋這首詩，」愛麗絲說，（就在剛剛幾分鐘內，她已經長得十分高大了，所以她完全不怕打斷國王的話。）「我願意給他三十塊錢。我認爲這些詩沒有任何意義。」

陪審員都在紙板上寫下：「她認爲這首詩沒有任何意義。」但是沒有任何一個想要解釋這首詩。

「如果這首詩沒有任何意義，」國王說：「那就簡單許多了。你知道，我們根本就不用麻煩想找出什麼意義，而且我也不懂什麼意義。」國王邊說邊把這首詩攤在膝上，用一隻眼睛瞄著，「不過，我好像看出一點端倪了──『說我不會游泳』──就是說你不會游泳的意思，是嗎？」國王對著紅心傑克說。

紅心傑克傷心地搖搖頭說：「我看起來像會游泳的樣子嗎？」（他當然不會游泳，因爲他全身是由硬紙片做成的。）

「這就對了，」國王一邊說，一邊又繼續自言自語地嘟囔著這些詩句，

「『我們都知道這是眞的』──這當然是指陪審團──『我給她一，他們給他

二』——這肯定是指那些被偷的水果塔，你看……」

「可是後面又寫『他們又從他那邊拿來還給你，』」愛麗絲說。

「喔，是啊，不就是這些東西嗎？」國王指著桌上的水果塔，得意地說：

「事情非常清楚了。再看：『在她還沒說「呸」之前』——親愛的，我想你沒

有說過『呸』吧？」他對皇后說。

「從來沒有！」皇后大發雷霆，說著就「呸」的一聲把桌上的墨水缸往蜥

蜴比爾身上扔去。倒楣的比爾已經不再用手指在紙板上寫字，牠發現那樣是寫

不出字的，不過現在臉上有了墨水，於是牠又急忙沾著臉上的墨水開始寫字。

「那麼這句話就和你不『配』了！」國王帶著微笑環視著法庭說。法庭上

鴉雀無聲。

「這是雙關語！」國王有點生氣地說，於是大家都笑了起來。「讓陪審員

做出裁決吧！」國王說道，這大概是他今天第二十次說這句話了。

「不，不，」皇后說，「應該先定罪，後裁決。」

「胡說八道！竟然要先定罪。」愛麗絲大聲說。

「你給我閉嘴！」皇后氣得臉色都發紫了。

「我才不要！」愛麗絲毫不示弱地回答。

「砍掉她的頭！」皇后聲嘶力竭地喊道。但是沒有人行動。

「誰管你？」愛麗絲說，這時她已經恢復到本來的身材了，「你們不過是一副紙牌！」

話一說完，整副撲克牌突然全部升至空中，朝她飛撲而來，她發出尖叫，

又氣又急，想用手撥開——卻突然發現自己躺在河岸邊，頭枕在姐姐的腿上，姐姐正在把從樹上飄落下來的枯葉撢掉。

「醒醒，愛麗絲！」

「啊，我做了個好奇怪的夢！」愛麗絲說道：「看，你睡了多久！」

姐——就是你剛才讀到的那些。」等她講完後，姐姐親了她一下說：「真的，真是個好奇怪的夢，親愛的，不過現在你先回去喝茶吧！時候不早了。」於是，愛麗絲起身跑開，腦中不斷想著，剛才那個夢多麼奇妙呀！

陽，想著小愛麗絲以及她夢中奇幻的經歷，自己也似乎進了夢境：

愛麗絲離開以後，姐姐仍靜靜地坐著，一隻手托著頭，凝望慢慢西下的夕

她先夢見小愛麗絲，一雙小手抱著膝蓋，用明亮而熱切的眼睛看著她——她聽到小愛麗絲說話的聲音，看到她微微擺頭、把不停飄到眼睛前的頭髮甩開的奇怪動作——而當她一直專注聽著四周聲音時（或說她似乎能聽見），身邊的一切似乎都隨著妹妹夢中那些奇異的動物活了過來。

那隻大白兔跳來跳去，於是腳下的草地沙沙作響──那隻嚇壞了的老鼠在鄰近的池塘游來游去，不時揚起一陣水花──她還聽到三月兔和牠的朋友坐在茶桌旁，共享沒完沒了的餐點時碰擊茶杯的聲音，還有皇后命令處決她的不幸客人的尖銳叫嚷聲──同時也聽到豬小孩在公爵夫人腿上打噴嚏，以及盤碗的摔碎聲──甚至也能聽見獅鷲的喊叫聲，蜥蜴寫字時的沙沙聲，那些被「制止」的豚鼠在袋中掙扎的聲音，混雜著遠處傳來的假海龜悲哀的抽泣聲，種種聲音充滿了四周。

她閉著眼睛坐著不動，好像自己也到了那個奇妙的世界，雖然她知道只要一睜開眼睛，就會回到乏味的現實世界──野草會沙沙作響只是因為被風吹拂，池水會有連漪不過是因為蘆葦擺動──茶杯的碰擊聲實際上是羊頸上的鈴鐺聲，皇后的尖叫聲其實是來自於牧童的呼喚聲──豬小孩的噴嚏聲、獅鷲的叫嚷聲和各種奇怪聲音，不過是繁忙季節時農村裡的各種喧鬧聲──而遠處耕牛的低吟成了夢中假海龜的哀泣聲。

最後，她開始想像她的小妹妹將如何長大成人；而儘管隨著時間過去，她仍然如童年般擁有一顆純真爛漫的赤子之心；以及她會如何聚集許多孩子、講許多奇異的故事給他們聽，她的故事裡或許也有這個多年前的奇幻夢境，孩子們的眼睛都變得明亮而熱切；她也會和孩子們共享單純的煩惱和快樂，同時永遠記得自己的童年生活以及快樂的夏日時光。

想一想

你也曾做過這種看似完全不合理但卻非常好玩的夢嗎？如果從來沒有的話，那麼你的夢都是什麼樣子的？

愛麗絲夢遊仙境

Alice's Adventures in Wonderland

中英雙語版

Lewis Carroll

Illustrated by John Tenniel
（原版約翰・田尼爾復刻手繪插圖）

晨星出版

ALICE'S
ADVENTURES IN WONDERLAND

CONTENTS

01 /

Down the Rabbit-Hole

Alice was beginning to get very tired of sitting by her sister on the bank, and of having nothing to do: once or twice she had peeped into the book her sister was reading, but it had no pictures or conversations in it, 'and what is the use of a book,' thought Alice 'without pictures or conversations?'

So she was considering in her own mind (as well as she could, for the hot day made her feel very sleepy and stupid), whether the pleasure of making a daisy-chain would be worth the trouble of getting up and picking the daisies, when suddenly a White Rabbit with pink eyes ran close by her.

There was nothing so *very* remarkable in that; nor did Alice think it so *very* much out of the way to hear the

Rabbit say to itself, 'Oh dear! Oh dear! I shall be late!' (when she thought it over afterwards, it occurred to her that she ought to have wondered at this, but at the time it all seemed quite natural); but when the Rabbit actually *took a watch out of its waistcoat-pocket*, and looked at it, and then hurried on, Alice started to her feet, for it flashed across her mind that she had never before seen a rabbit with either a waistcoat-pocket, or a watch to take out of it, and burning with curiosity, she ran across the field after it, and fortunately was just in time to see it pop down a large rabbit-hole under the hedge.

In another moment down went Alice after it, never once considering how in the world she was to get out again.

The rabbit-hole went straight on like a tunnel for some way, and then dipped suddenly down, so suddenly that Alice had not a moment to think about stopping herself before she found herself falling down a very deep well.

Either the well was very deep, or she fell very slowly, for she had plenty of time as she went down to look about her and to wonder what was going to happen next.

waistcoat [ˈwestˌkot] *n* 背心

First, she tried to look down and make out what she was coming to, but it was too dark to see anything; then she looked at the sides of the well, and noticed that they were filled with cupboards and book-shelves; here and there she saw maps and pictures hung upon pegs. She took down a jar from one of the shelves as she passed; it was labelled 'ORANGE MARMALADE', but to her great disappointment it was empty: she did not like to drop the jar for fear of killing somebody, so managed to put it into one of the cupboards as she fell past it.

'Well!' thought Alice to herself, 'after such a fall as this, I shall think nothing of tumbling down stairs! How brave they'll all think me at home! Why, I wouldn't say anything about it, even if I fell off the top of the house!' (Which was very likely true.)

Down, down, down. Would the fall *never* come to an end! 'I wonder how many miles I've fallen by this time?' she said aloud. 'I must be getting somewhere near the centre of the earth. Let me see: that would be four thousand miles down, I think—' (for, you see, Alice had learnt several things of this sort in her lessons in the schoolroom, and though this was not a *very*good

marmalade ['mɑrml̩ˌed] *n* 橘子（或檸檬）果醬

opportunity for showing off her knowledge, as there was no one to listen to her, still it was good practice to say it over) '—yes, that's about the right distance—but then I wonder what Latitude or Longitude I've got to?' (Alice had no idea what Latitude was, or Longitude either, but thought they were nice grand words to say.)

Presently she began again. 'I wonder if I shall fall right *through* the earth! How funny it'll seem to come out among the people that walk with their heads downward! The Antipathies, I think—' (she was rather glad there *was* no one listening, this time, as it didn't sound at all the right word) '—but I shall have to ask them what the name of the country is, you know. Please, Ma'am, is this New Zealand or Australia?' (and she tried to curtsey as she spoke—fancy *curtseying* as you're falling through the air! Do you think you could manage it?) 'And what an ignorant little girl she'll think me for asking! No, it'll never do to ask: perhaps I shall see it written up somewhere.'

Down, down, down. There was nothing else to do, so Alice soon began talking again. 'Dinah'll miss me very

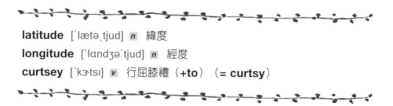

latitude [ˈlætəˌtjud] *n* 緯度
longitude [ˈlɑndʒəˈtjud] *n* 經度
curtsey [ˈkɝtsɪ] *v* 行屈膝禮（**+to**）（**= curtsy**）

much to-night, I should think!' (Dinah was the cat.) 'I hope they'll remember her saucer of milk at tea-time. Dinah my dear! I wish you were down here with me! There are no mice in the air, I'm afraid, but you might catch a bat, and that's very like a mouse, you know. But do cats eat bats, I wonder?' And here Alice began to get rather sleepy, and went on saying to herself, in a dreamy sort of way, 'Do cats eat bats? Do cats eat bats?' and sometimes, 'Do bats eat cats?' for, you see, as she couldn't answer either question, it didn't much matter which way she put it. She felt that she was dozing off, and had just begun to dream that she was walking hand in hand with Dinah, and saying to her very earnestly, 'Now, Dinah, tell me the truth: did you ever eat a bat?' when suddenly, thump! thump! down she came upon a heap of sticks and dry leaves, and the fall was over.

Alice was not a bit hurt, and she jumped up on to her feet in a moment: she looked up, but it was all dark overhead; before her was another long passage, and the White Rabbit was still in sight, hurrying down it. There was not a moment to be lost: away went Alice like the wind, and was just in time to hear it say, as it turned a corner, 'Oh my ears and whiskers, how late it's getting!' She was close behind it when she turned the corner, but the Rabbit was no longer to be seen: she found herself in a long, low hall, which was lit up by a row of lamps

hanging from the roof.

There were doors all round the hall, but they were all locked; and when Alice had been all the way down one side and up the other, trying every door, she walked sadly down the middle, wondering how she was ever to get out again.

Suddenly she came upon a little three-legged table, all made of solid glass; there was nothing on it except a tiny golden key, and Alice's first thought was that it might belong to one of the doors of the hall; but, alas! either the locks were too large, or the key was too small, but at any rate it would not open any of them. However, on the second time round, she came upon a low curtain she had not noticed before, and behind it was a little door about fifteen inches high: she tried the little golden key in the lock, and to her great delight it fitted!

Alice opened the door and found that it led into a small passage, not much larger than a rat-hole: she knelt down and looked along the passage into the loveliest garden you ever saw. How she longed to get out of that

dark hall, and wander about among those beds of bright flowers and those cool fountains, but she could not even get her head through the doorway; 'and even if my head would go through,' thought poor Alice, 'it would be of very little use without my shoulders. Oh, how I wish I could shut up like a telescope! I think I could, if I only knew how to begin.' For, you see, so many out-of-the-way things had happened lately, that Alice had begun to think that very few things indeed were really impossible.

There seemed to be no use in waiting by the little door, so she went back to the table, half hoping she might find another key on it, or at any rate a book of rules for shutting people up like telescopes: this time she found a little bottle on it, ('which certainly was not here before,' said Alice,) and round the neck of the bottle was a paper label,

telescope [ˈtɛləˌskop] *n* （單筒）望遠鏡

with the words 'DRINK ME' beautifully printed on it in large letters.

It was all very well to say 'Drink me,' but the wise little Alice was not going to do *that* in a hurry. 'No, I'll look first,' she said, 'and see whether it's marked "poison" or not'; for she had read several nice little histories about children who had got burnt, and eaten up by wild beasts and other unpleasant things, all because they *would* not remember the simple rules their friends had taught them: such as, that a red-hot poker will burn you if you hold it too long; and that if you cut your finger *very* deeply with a knife, it usually bleeds; and she had never forgotten that, if you drink much from a bottle marked 'poison,' it is almost certain to disagree with you, sooner or later.

However, this bottle was *not* marked 'poison,' so Alice ventured to taste it, and finding it very nice, (it had, in fact, a sort of mixed flavour of cherry-tart, custard, pine-apple, roast turkey, toffee, and hot buttered toast,) she very soon finished it off.

♠ ♥ ♣ ♦

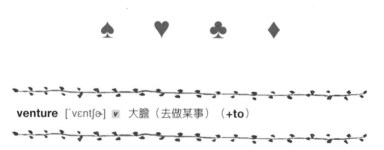

venture [ˈvɛntʃə] **v** 大膽（去做某事）（**+to**）

'What a curious feeling!' said Alice; 'I must be shutting up like a telescope.'

And so it was indeed: she was now only ten inches high, and her face brightened up at the thought that she was now the right size for going through the little door into that lovely garden. First, however, she waited for a few minutes to see if she was going to shrink any further: she felt a little nervous about this; 'for it might end, you know,' said Alice to herself, 'in my going out altogether, like a candle. I wonder what I should be like then?' And she tried to fancy what the flame of a candle is like after the candle is blown out, for she could not remember ever having seen such a thing.

After a while, finding that nothing more happened, she decided on going into the garden at once; but, alas for poor Alice! when she got to the door, she found she had forgotten the little golden key, and when she went back to the table for it, she found she could not possibly reach it: she could see it quite plainly through the glass, and she tried her best to climb up one of the legs of the table, but it was too slippery; and when she had tired herself out with trying, the poor little thing sat down and cried.

'Come, there's no use in crying like that!' said Alice to herself, rather sharply; 'I advise you to leave off this minute!' She generally gave herself very good advice, (though she very seldom followed it), and sometimes she

scolded herself so severely as to bring tears into her eyes; and once she remembered trying to box her own ears for having cheated herself in a game of croquet she was playing against herself, for this curious child was very fond of pretending to be two people. 'But it's no use now,' thought poor Alice, 'to pretend to be two people! Why, there's hardly enough of me left to make *one* respectable person!'

Soon her eye fell on a little glass box that was lying under the table: she opened it, and found in it a very small cake, on which the words 'EAT ME' were beautifully marked in currants. 'Well, I'll eat it,' said Alice, 'and if it makes me grow larger, I can reach the key; and if it makes me grow smaller, I can creep under the door; so either way I'll get into the garden, and I don't care which happens!'

She ate a little bit, and said anxiously to herself, 'Which way? Which way?', holding her hand on the top of her head to feel which way it was growing, and she was quite surprised to find that she remained the same size: to be sure, this generally happens when one eats cake, but Alice had got so much into the way of expecting nothing

scold [skold] **v** 責罵；嘮嘮叨叨地責備

but out-of-the-way things to happen, that it seemed quite dull and stupid for life to go on in the common way.

So she set to work, and very soon finished off the cake.

The Pool of Tears

'Curiouser and curiouser!' cried Alice (she was so much surprised, that for the moment she quite forgot how to speak good English); 'now I'm opening out like the largest telescope that ever was! Good-bye, feet!' (for when she looked down at her feet, they seemed to be almost out of sight, they were getting so far off). 'Oh, my poor little feet, I wonder who will put on your shoes and stockings for you now, dears? I'm sure *I* shan't be able! I shall be a great deal too far off to trouble myself about you: you must manage the best way you can;—but I must be kind to

them,' thought Alice, 'or perhaps they won't walk the way I want to go! Let me see: I'll give them a new pair of boots every Christmas.'

And she went on planning to herself how she would manage it. 'They must go by the carrier,' she thought; 'and how funny it'll seem, sending presents to one's own feet! And how odd the directions will look!

Alice's Right Foot, Esq.

Hearthrug,

near The Fender,

(with Alice's love).

Oh dear, what nonsense I'm talking!'

Just then her head struck against the roof of the hall: in fact she was now more than nine feet high, and she at once took up the little golden key and hurried off to the garden door.

Poor Alice! It was as much as she could do, lying down on one side, to look through into the garden with one eye; but to get through was more hopeless than ever: she sat down and began to cry again.

'You ought to be ashamed of yourself,' said Alice, 'a great girl like you,' (she might well say this), 'to go on crying in this way! Stop this moment, I tell you!' But she went on all the same, shedding gallons of tears, until there was a large pool all round her, about four inches deep and reaching half down the hall.

After a time she heard a little pattering of feet in the distance, and she hastily dried her eyes to see what was coming. It was the White Rabbit returning, splendidly dressed, with a pair of white kid gloves in one hand and a large fan in the other: he came trotting along in a great hurry, muttering to  himself as he came, 'Oh! the Duchess, the Duchess! Oh! won't she be savage if I've kept her waiting!' Alice felt so desperate that she was ready to ask help of any one; so, when the Rabbit came near her, she began, in a low, timid voice, 'If you please, sir—' The Rabbit started violently, dropped the white kid gloves and the fan, and skurried away into the darkness as hard as he could go.

Alice took up the fan and gloves, and, as the hall was very hot, she kept fanning herself all the time she went on

savage [ˈsævɪdʒ] *adj* 狂怒的

talking: 'Dear, dear! How queer everything is to-day! And yesterday things went on just as usual. I wonder if I've been changed in the night? Let me think: was I the same when I got up this morning? I almost think I can remember feeling a little different. But if I'm not the same, the next question is, Who in the world am I? Ah, *that's* the great puzzle!' And she began thinking over all the children she knew that were of the same age as herself, to see if she could have been changed for any of them.

'I'm sure I'm not Ada,' she said, 'for her hair goes in such long ringlets, and mine doesn't go in ringlets at all; and I'm sure I can't be Mabel, for I know all sorts of things, and she, oh! she knows such a very little! Besides, *she's* she, and *I'm* I, and—oh dear, how puzzling it all is! I'll try if I know all the things I used to know. Let me see: four times five is twelve, and four times six is thirteen, and four times seven is—oh dear! I shall never get to twenty at that rate! However, the Multiplication Table doesn't signify: let's try Geography. London is the capital of Paris, and Paris is the capital of Rome, and Rome—no, *that's* all wrong, I'm certain! I must have been changed for Mabel! I'll try and say "*How doth the little*—"' and she crossed her

signify [ˈsɪgnəˌfaɪ] **v** （通常用於否定句或疑問句）有重要性

hands on her lap as if she were saying lessons, and began to repeat it, but her voice sounded hoarse and strange, and the words did not come the same as they used to do:—

'How doth the little crocodile
Improve his shining tail,
And pour the waters of the Nile
On every golden scale!

'How cheerfully he seems to grin,
How neatly spread his claws,
And welcome little fishes in
With gently smiling jaws!'

'I'm sure those are not the right words,' said poor Alice, and her eyes filled with tears again as she went on, 'I must be Mabel after all, and I shall have to go and live in that poky little house, and have next to no toys to play with, and oh! ever so many lessons to learn! No, I've made up my mind about it; if I'm Mabel, I'll stay down here! It'll be no use their putting their heads down and saying "Come up again, dear!" I shall only look up and say "Who am I then? Tell me that first, and then, if I like being that person, I'll come up: if not, I'll stay down here till I'm somebody else"—but, oh dear!' cried Alice, with a sudden burst of tears, 'I do wish they *would* put their heads down! I am so *very* tired of being all alone here!'

As she said this she looked down at her hands, and was surprised to see that she had put on one of the Rabbit's little white kid gloves while she was talking. 'How *can* I have done that?' she thought. 'I must be growing small again.' She got up and went to the table to measure herself by it, and found that, as nearly as she could guess, she was now about two feet high, and was going on shrinking rapidly: she soon found out that the cause of this was the fan she was holding, and she dropped it hastily, just in time to avoid shrinking away altogether.

'That *was* a narrow escape!' said Alice, a good deal frightened at the sudden change, but very glad to find herself still in existence; 'and now for the garden!' and she ran with all speed back to the little door: but, alas! the little door was shut again, and the little golden key was lying on the glass table as before, 'and things are worse than ever,' thought the poor child, 'for I never was so small as this before, never! And I declare it's too bad, that it is!'

As she said these words her foot slipped, and in another moment, splash! she was up to her chin in salt water. Her first idea was that she had somehow fallen into the sea, 'and in that case I can go back by railway,' she said to herself. (Alice had been to the seaside once in her life, and had come to the general conclusion, that wherever you go to on the English coast you find a number of bathing machines in the sea, some children digging in the

sand with wooden spades, then a row of lodging houses, and behind them a railway station.) However, she soon made out that she was in the pool of tears which she had wept when she was nine feet high.

'I wish I hadn't cried so much!' said Alice, as she swam about, trying to find her way out. 'I shall be punished for it now, I suppose, by being drowned in my own tears! That *will* be a queer thing, to be sure! However, everything is queer to-day.'

Just then she heard something splashing about in the pool a little way off, and she swam nearer to make out what it was: at first she thought it must be a walrus or hippopotamus, but then she remembered how small she was now, and she soon made out that it was only a mouse that had slipped in like herself.

'Would it be of any use, now,' thought Alice, 'to speak to this mouse? Everything is so out-of-the-way down here, that I should think very likely it can talk: at any rate, there's no harm in trying.' So she began: 'O Mouse, do you know the way out of this pool? I am very tired of

swimming about here, O Mouse!' (Alice thought this must be the right way of speaking to a mouse: she had never done such a thing before, but she remembered having seen in her brother's Latin Grammar, 'A mouse—of a mouse—to a mouse—a mouse—O mouse!') The Mouse looked at her rather inquisitively, and seemed to her to wink with one of its little eyes, but it said nothing.

'Perhaps it doesn't understand English,' thought Alice; 'I daresay it's a French mouse, come over with William the Conqueror.' (For, with all her knowledge of history, Alice had no very clear notion how long ago anything had happened.) So she began again: 'Ou est ma chatte?' which was the first sentence in her French lesson-book. The Mouse gave a sudden leap out of the water, and seemed to quiver all over with fright. 'Oh, I beg your

pardon!' cried Alice hastily, afraid that she had hurt the poor animal's feelings. 'I quite forgot you didn't like cats.'

'Not like cats!' cried the Mouse, in a shrill, passionate voice. 'Would *you* like cats if you were me?'

'Well, perhaps not,' said Alice in a soothing tone: 'don't be angry about it. And yet I wish I could show you our cat Dinah: I think you'd take a fancy to cats if you could only see her. She is such a dear quiet thing,' Alice went on, half to herself, as she swam lazily about in the pool, 'and she sits purring so nicely by the fire, licking her paws and washing her face—and she is such a nice soft thing to nurse—and she's such a capital one for catching mice—oh, I beg your pardon!' cried Alice again, for this time the Mouse was bristling all over, and she felt certain it must be really offended. 'We won't talk about her any more if you'd rather not.'

'We indeed!' cried the Mouse, who was trembling down to the end of his tail. 'As if *I* would talk on such a subject! Our family always *hated* cats: nasty, low, vulgar

shrill [ʃrɪl] *adj* 尖聲的，刺耳的
passionate [ˈpæʃənɪt] *adj* 激昂的；生氣的
offended [əˈfɛndɪd] *adj* 被冒犯的
vulgar [ˈvʌlgɚ] *adj* 下流的

things! Don't let me hear the name again!'

'I won't indeed!' said Alice, in a great hurry to change the subject of conversation. 'Are you—are you fond—of—of dogs?' The Mouse did not answer, so Alice went on eagerly: 'There is such a nice little dog near our house I should like to show you! A little bright-eyed terrier, you know, with oh, such long curly brown hair! And it'll fetch things when you throw them, and it'll sit up and beg for its dinner, and all sorts of things—I can't remember half of them—and it belongs to a farmer, you know, and he says it's so useful, it's worth a hundred pounds! He says it kills all the rats and—oh dear!' cried Alice in a sorrowful tone, 'I'm afraid I've offended it again!' For the Mouse was swimming away from her as hard as it could go, and making quite a commotion in the pool as it went.

So she called softly after it, 'Mouse dear! Do come back again, and we won't talk about cats or dogs either, if you don't like them!' When the Mouse heard this, it turned round and swam slowly back to her: its face was quite pale (with passion, Alice thought), and it said in a low trembling voice, 'Let us get to the shore, and then I'll tell

commotion [kəˈmoʃən] *n* 騷動，喧鬧
pale [pel] *adj* 蒼白的，慘白的

you my history, and you'll understand why it is I hate cats and dogs.'

It was high time to go, for the pool was getting quite crowded with the birds and animals that had fallen into it: there were a Duck and a Dodo, a Lory and an Eaglet, and several other curious creatures. Alice led the way, and the whole party swam to the shore.

03 /

A Caucus-Race and a Long Tale

They were indeed a queer-looking party that assembled on the bank—the birds with draggled feathers, the animals with their fur clinging close to them, and all dripping wet, cross, and uncomfortable.

The first question of course was, how to get dry again: they had a consultation about this, and after a few minutes it seemed quite natural to Alice to find herself talking familiarly with them, as if she had known them all her life. Indeed, she had quite a long argument with the Lory, who at last turned sulky, and would only say, 'I am older than you, and must know better'; and this Alice would not allow without knowing how old it was, and, as the Lory positively refused to tell its age, there was no more to be said.

consultation [ˌkɑnsəlˈteʃən] **n** （磋商）會議

At last the Mouse, who seemed to be a person of authority among them, called out, 'Sit down, all of you, and listen to me! *I'll* soon make you dry enough!' They all sat down at once, in a large ring, with the Mouse in the middle. Alice kept her eyes anxiously fixed on it, for she felt sure she would catch a bad cold if she did not get dry very soon.

'Ahem!' said the Mouse with an important air, 'are you all ready? This is the driest thing I know. Silence all round, if you please! "William the Conqueror, whose cause was favoured by the pope, was soon submitted to by the English, who wanted leaders, and had been of late

much accustomed to usurpation and conquest. Edwin and Morcar, the earls of Mercia and Northumbria—"'

'Ugh!' said the Lory, with a shiver.

'I beg your pardon!' said the Mouse, frowning, but very politely: 'Did you speak?'

'Not I!' said the Lory hastily.

'I thought you did,' said the Mouse. '—I proceed. "Edwin and Morcar, the earls of Mercia and Northumbria, declared for him: and even Stigand, the patriotic archbishop of Canterbury, found it advisable—"'

'Found *what*?' said the Duck.

'Found *it*,' the Mouse replied rather crossly: 'of course you know what "it" means.'

'I know what "it" means well enough, when *I* find a thing,' said the Duck: 'it's generally a frog or a worm. The question is, what did the archbishop find?'

The Mouse did not notice this question, but hurriedly went on, '"—found it advisable to go with Edgar Atheling to meet William and offer him the crown. William's conduct at first was moderate. But the insolence of his

usurpation [ˌjuzə-ˈpeʃən] *n* 篡奪；奪取；侵佔
conquest [ˈkɑŋkwɛst] *n* 征服；佔領
insolence [ˈɪnsələns] *n* 傲慢；無禮

Normans—" How are you getting on now, my dear?' it continued, turning to Alice as it spoke.

'As wet as ever,' said Alice in a melancholy tone: 'it doesn't seem to dry me at all.'

'In that case,' said the Dodo solemnly, rising to its feet, 'I move that the meeting adjourn, for the immediate adoption of more energetic remedies—'

'Speak English!' said the Eaglet. 'I don't know the meaning of half those long words, and, what's more, I don't believe you do either!' And the Eaglet bent down its head to hide a smile: some of the other birds tittered audibly.

'What I was going to say,' said the Dodo in an offended tone, 'was, that the best thing to get us dry would be a Caucus-race.'

'What *is* a Caucus-race?' said Alice; not that she wanted much to know, but the Dodo had paused as if it thought that *somebody* ought to speak, and no one else

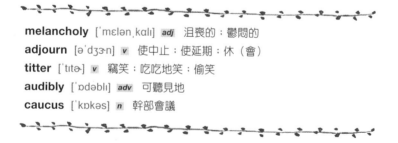

melancholy [ˈmɛlənˌkɑlɪ] *adj* 沮喪的；鬱悶的
adjourn [əˈdʒɜˑn] *v* 使中止；使延期；休（會）
titter [ˈtɪtə-] *v* 竊笑；吃吃地笑；偷笑
audibly [ˈɒdəblɪ] *adv* 可聽見地
caucus [ˈkɒkəs] *n* 幹部會議

seemed inclined to say anything.

'Why,' said the Dodo, 'the best way to explain it is to do it.' (And, as you might like to try the thing yourself, some winter day, I will tell you how the Dodo managed it.)

First it marked out a race-course, in a sort of circle, ('the exact shape doesn't matter,' it said,) and then all the party were placed along the course, here and there. There was no 'One, two, three, and away,' but they began running when they liked, and left off when they liked, so that it was not easy to know when the race was over. However, when they had been running half an hour or so, and were quite dry again, the Dodo suddenly called out 'The race is over!' and they all crowded round it, panting, and asking, 'But who has won?'

This question the Dodo could not answer without a great deal of thought, and it sat for a long time with one finger pressed upon its forehead (the position in which you usually see Shakespeare, in the pictures of him), while the rest waited in silence. At last the Dodo said, '*Everybody* has won, and all must have prizes.'

'But who is to give the prizes?' quite a chorus of voices asked.

exact [ɪɡˈzækt] *adj* 確切的，精確的

'Why, *she*, of course,' said the Dodo, pointing to Alice with one finger; and the whole party at once crowded round her, calling out in a confused way, 'Prizes! Prizes!'

Alice had no idea what to do, and in despair she put her hand in her pocket, and pulled out a box of comfits, (luckily the salt water had not got into it), and handed them round as prizes. There was exactly one a-piece all round.

'But she must have a prize herself, you know,' said the Mouse.

'Of course,' the Dodo replied very gravely. 'What else have you got in your pocket?' he went on, turning to Alice.

'Only a thimble,' said Alice sadly.

'Hand it over here,' said the Dodo.

Then they all crowded round her once more, while the Dodo solemnly presented the thimble, saying 'We beg your acceptance of this elegant thimble'; and, when it had finished this short speech, they all cheered.

Alice thought the whole thing very absurd, but they

all looked so grave that she did not dare to laugh; and, as she could not think of anything to say, she simply bowed, and took the thimble, looking as solemn as she could.

The next thing was to eat the comfits: this caused some noise and confusion, as the large birds complained that they could not taste theirs, and the small ones choked and had to be patted on the back. However, it was over at last, and they sat down again in a ring, and begged the Mouse to tell them something more.

'You promised to tell me your history, you know,' said Alice, 'and why it is you hate—C and D,' she added in a whisper, half afraid that it would be offended again.

'Mine is a long and a sad tale!' said the Mouse, turning to Alice, and sighing.

'It *is* a long tail, certainly,' said Alice, looking down with wonder at the Mouse's tail; 'but why do you call it sad?' And she kept on puzzling about it while the Mouse was speaking, so that her idea of the tale was something like this:—

> *'Fury said to a*
> *mouse, That he*
> *met in the*
> *house,*
> *"Let us*
> *both go to*
> *law: I will*
> *prosecute*

you.—Come,
I'll take no
denial; We
must have a
trial: For
really this
morning I've
nothing
to do."
Said the
mouse to the
cur, "Such
a trial,
dear Sir,
With
no jury
or judge,
would be
wasting
our
breath."
"I'll be
judge, I'll
be jury,"
Said
cunning

old Fury:
"I'll
try the
whole
cause,
and
condemn
you
to
death."'

'You are not attending!' said the Mouse to Alice severely. 'What are you thinking of?'

'I beg your pardon,' said Alice very humbly: 'you had got to the fifth bend, I think?'

'I had *not!*' cried the Mouse, sharply and very angrily.

'A knot!' said Alice, always ready to make herself useful, and looking anxiously about her. 'Oh, do let me help to undo it!'

'I shall do nothing of the sort,' said the Mouse, getting up and walking away. 'You insult me by talking such nonsense!'

'I didn't mean it!' pleaded poor Alice. 'But you're so

plead [plid] **v** 抗辯，辯護

easily offended, you know!'

The Mouse only growled in reply.

'Please come back and finish your story!' Alice called after it; and the others all joined in chorus, 'Yes, please do!' but the Mouse only shook its head impatiently, and walked a little quicker.

'What a pity it wouldn't stay!' sighed the Lory, as soon as it was quite out of sight; and an old Crab took the opportunity of saying to her daughter 'Ah, my dear! Let this be a lesson to you never to lose *your* temper!' 'Hold your tongue, Ma!' said the young Crab, a little snappishly. 'You're enough to try the patience of an oyster!'

'I wish I had our Dinah here, I know I do!' said Alice aloud, addressing nobody in particular. 'She'd soon fetch it back!'

'And who is Dinah, if I might venture to ask the question?' said the Lory.

Alice replied eagerly, for she was always ready to talk about her pet: 'Dinah's our cat. And she's such a capital one for catching mice you can't think! And oh, I wish you could see her after the birds! Why, she'll eat a little bird as soon as look at it!'

This speech caused a remarkable sensation among the party. Some of the birds hurried off at once: one old Magpie began wrapping itself up very carefully, remarking, 'I really must be getting home; the night-air

doesn't suit my throat!' and a Canary called out in a trembling voice to its children, 'Come away, my dears! It's high time you were all in bed!' On various pretexts they all moved off, and Alice was soon left alone.

'I wish I hadn't mentioned Dinah!' she said to herself in a melancholy tone. 'Nobody seems to like her, down here, and I'm sure she's the best cat in the world! Oh, my dear Dinah! I wonder if I shall ever see you any more!' And here poor Alice began to cry again, for she felt very lonely and low-spirited. In a little while, however, she again heard a little pattering of footsteps in the distance, and she looked up eagerly, half hoping that the Mouse had changed his mind, and was coming back to finish his story.

pretext [ˈpritɛkst] *n* 藉口；託辭

The Rabbit Sends in a Little Bill

It was the White Rabbit, trotting slowly back again, and looking anxiously about as it went, as if it had lost something; and she heard it muttering to itself 'The Duchess! The Duchess! Oh my dear paws! Oh my fur and whiskers! She'll get me executed, as sure as ferrets are ferrets! Where *can* I have dropped them, I wonder?' Alice guessed in a moment that it was looking for the fan and the pair of white kid gloves, and she very good-naturedly began hunting about for them, but they were nowhere to be seen—everything seemed to have changed since her swim in the pool, and the great hall, with the glass table and the little door, had vanished completely.

Very soon the Rabbit noticed Alice, as she went hunting about, and called out to her in an angry tone, 'Why, Mary Ann, what *are* you doing out here? Run home this moment, and fetch me a pair of gloves and a fan! Quick, now!' And Alice was so much frightened that she ran off at once in the direction it pointed to, without

trying to explain the mistake it had made.

'He took me for his housemaid,' she said to herself as she ran. 'How surprised he'll be when he finds out who I am! But I'd better take him his fan and gloves—that is, if I can find them.' As she said this, she came upon a neat little house, on the door of which was a bright brass plate with the name 'W. RABBIT' engraved upon it. She went in without knocking, and hurried upstairs, in great fear lest she should meet the real Mary Ann, and be turned out of the house before she had found the fan and gloves.

'How queer it seems,' Alice said to herself, 'to be going messages for a rabbit! I suppose Dinah'll be sending me on messages next!' And she began fancying the sort of thing that would happen: '"Miss Alice! Come here directly, and get ready for your walk!" "Coming in a minute, nurse! But I've got to see that the mouse doesn't get out." Only I don't think,' Alice went on, 'that they'd let Dinah stop in the house if it began ordering people about like that!'

By this time she had found her way into a tidy little room with a table in the window, and on it (as she had hoped) a fan and two or three pairs of tiny white kid gloves: she took up the fan and a pair of the gloves, and was just going to leave the room, when her eye fell upon a little bottle that stood near the looking-glass. There was no label this time with the words 'DRINK ME,' but nevertheless she uncorked it and put it to her lips. 'I know

something interesting is sure to happen,' she said to herself, 'whenever I eat or drink anything; so I'll just see what this bottle does. I do hope it'll make me grow large again, for really I'm quite tired of being such a tiny little thing!'

It did so indeed, and much sooner than she had expected: before she had drunk half the bottle, she found her head pressing against the ceiling, and had to stoop to save her neck from being broken. She hastily put down the bottle, saying to herself 'That's quite enough—I hope I shan't grow any more—As it is, I can't get out at the door—I do wish I hadn't drunk quite so much!'

Alas! it was too late to wish that! She went on growing, and growing, and very soon had to kneel down on the

floor: in another minute there was not even room for this, and she tried the effect of lying down with one elbow against the door, and the other arm curled round her head. Still she went on growing, and, as a last resource, she put one arm out of the window, and one foot up the chimney, and said to herself 'Now I can do no more, whatever happens. What *will* become of me?'

Luckily for Alice, the little magic bottle had now had its full effect, and she grew no larger: still it was very uncomfortable, and, as there seemed to be no sort of chance of her ever getting out of the room again, no wonder she felt unhappy.

'It was much pleasanter at home,' thought poor Alice, 'when one wasn't always growing larger and smaller, and being ordered about by mice and rabbits. I almost wish I hadn't gone down that rabbit-hole—and yet—and yet— it's rather curious, you know, this sort of life! I do wonder what *can* have happened to me! When I used to read fairy-tales, I fancied that kind of thing never happened, and now here I am in the middle of one! There ought to be a book written about me, that there ought! And when I grow up, I'll write one—but I'm grown up now,' she added in a sorrowful tone; 'at least there's no room to grow up any more *here*.'

'But then,' thought Alice, 'shall I *never* get any older than I am now? That'll be a comfort, one way—never to

be an old woman—but then—always to have lessons to learn! Oh, I shouldn't like *that*!'

'Oh, you foolish Alice!' she answered herself. 'How can you learn lessons in here? Why, there's hardly room for *you*, and no room at all for any lesson-books!'

And so she went on, taking first one side and then the other, and making quite a conversation of it altogether; but after a few minutes she heard a voice outside, and stopped to listen.

'Mary Ann! Mary Ann!' said the voice. 'Fetch me my gloves this moment!' Then came a little pattering of feet on the stairs. Alice knew it was the Rabbit coming to look for her, and she trembled till she shook the house, quite forgetting that she was now about a thousand times as large as the Rabbit, and had no reason to be afraid of it.

Presently the Rabbit came up to the door, and tried to open it; but, as the door opened inwards, and Alice's elbow was pressed hard against it, that attempt proved a failure. Alice heard it say to itself 'Then I'll go round and get in at the window.'

'*That* you won't' thought Alice, and, after waiting till she fancied she heard the Rabbit just under the window, she suddenly spread out her hand, and made a snatch in the air. She did not get hold of anything, but she heard a

little shriek and a fall, and a crash of broken glass, from which she concluded that it was just possible it had fallen into a cucumber-frame, or something of the sort.

Next came an angry voice—the Rabbit's—'Pat! Pat! Where are you?' And then a voice she had never heard before, 'Sure then I'm here! Digging for apples, yer honour!'

'Digging for apples, indeed!' said the Rabbit angrily. 'Here! Come and help me out of *this*!' (Sounds of more broken glass.)

'Now tell me, Pat, what's that in the window?'

'Sure, it's an arm, yer honour!' (He pronounced it 'arrum.')

'An arm, you goose! Who ever saw one that size? Why, it fills the whole window!'

'Sure, it does, yer honour: but it's an arm for all that.'

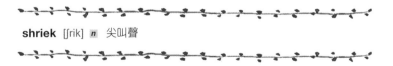

shriek [ʃrik] *n* 尖叫聲

'Well, it's got no business there, at any rate: go and take it away!'

There was a long silence after this, and Alice could only hear whispers now and then; such as, 'Sure, I don't like it, yer honour, at all, at all!' 'Do as I tell you, you coward!' and at last she spread out her hand again, and made another snatch in the air. This time there were *two* little shrieks, and more sounds of broken glass. 'What a number of cucumber-frames there must be!' thought Alice. 'I wonder what they'll do next! As for pulling me out of the window, I only wish they *could*! I'm sure *I* don't want to stay in here any longer!'

She waited for some time without hearing anything more: at last came a rumbling of little cartwheels, and the sound of a good many voices all talking together: she made out the words: 'Where's the other ladder?—Why, I hadn't to bring but one; Bill's got the other—Bill! fetch it here, lad!—Here, put 'em up at this corner—No, tie 'em together first—they don't reach half high enough yet— Oh! they'll do well enough; don't be particular—Here, Bill! catch hold of this rope—Will the roof bear?—Mind that loose slate—Oh, it's coming down! Heads below!' (a loud crash)—'Now, who did that?—It was Bill, I fancy—Who's to go down the chimney?—Nay, *I* shan't! *You* do it!—*That* I won't, then!—Bill's to go down—Here, Bill! the master says you're to go down the chimney!'

'Oh! So Bill's got to come down the chimney, has he?' said Alice to herself. 'Shy, they seem to put everything upon Bill! I wouldn't be in Bill's place for a good deal: this fireplace is narrow, to be sure; but I *think* I can kick a little!'

She drew her foot as far down the chimney as she could, and waited till she heard a little animal (she couldn't guess of what sort it was) scratching and scrambling about in the chimney close above her: then, saying to herself 'This is Bill,' she gave one sharp kick, and waited to see what would happen next.

The first thing she heard was a general chorus of 'There goes Bill!' then the Rabbit's

chimney [ˈtʃɪmnɪ] *n* 煙囪

voice along—'Catch him, you by the hedge!' then silence, and then another confusion of voices—'Hold up his head—Brandy now—Don't choke him—How was it, old fellow? What happened to you? Tell us all about it!'

Last came a little feeble, squeaking voice, ('That's Bill,' thought Alice,) 'Well, I hardly know—No more, thank ye; I'm better now—but I'm a deal too flustered to tell you— all I know is, something comes at me like a Jack-in-the-box, and up I goes like a sky-rocket!'

'So you did, old fellow!' said the others.

'We must burn the house down!' said the Rabbit's voice; and Alice called out as loud as she could, 'If you do, I'll set Dinah at you!'

There was a dead silence instantly, and Alice thought to herself, 'I wonder what they *will* do next! If they had any sense, they'd take the roof off.' After a minute or two, they began moving about again, and Alice heard the Rabbit say, 'A barrowful will do, to begin with.'

'A barrowful of *what?*' thought Alice; but she had not long to doubt, for the next moment a shower of little pebbles came rattling in at the window, and some of them

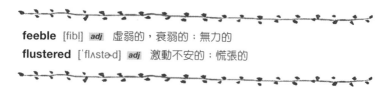

feeble [fibl] *adj* 虛弱的，衰弱的；無力的
flustered [ˈflʌstə-d] *adj* 激動不安的；慌張的

hit her in the face. 'I'll put a stop to this,' she said to herself, and shouted out, 'You'd better not do that again!' which produced another dead silence.

Alice noticed with some surprise that the pebbles were all turning into little cakes as they lay on the floor, and a bright idea came into her head. 'If I eat one of these cakes,' she thought, 'it's sure to make *some* change in my size; and as it can't possibly make me larger, it must make me smaller, I suppose.'

So she swallowed one of the cakes, and was delighted to find that she began shrinking directly. As soon as she was small enough to get through the door, she ran out of the house, and found quite a crowd of little animals and birds waiting outside. The poor little Lizard, Bill, was in the middle, being held up by two guinea-pigs, who were giving it something out of a bottle. They all made a rush at Alice the moment she appeared; but she ran off as hard as she could, and soon found herself safe in a thick wood.

'The first thing I've got to do,' said Alice to herself, as she wandered about in the wood, 'is to grow to my right size again; and the second thing is to find my way into that lovely garden. I think that will be the best plan.'

It sounded an excellent plan, no doubt, and very neatly and simply arranged; the only difficulty was, that she had not the smallest idea how to set about it; and while she was peering about anxiously among the trees, a little sharp

bark just over her head made her look up in a great hurry.

An enormous puppy was looking down at her with large round eyes, and feebly stretching out one paw, trying to touch her. 'Poor little thing!' said Alice, in a coaxing

coaxing [ˈkoksɪŋ] _adj_ 哄勸的

tone, and she tried hard to whistle to it; but she was terribly frightened all the time at the thought that it might be hungry, in which case it would be very likely to eat her up in spite of all her coaxing.

Hardly knowing what she did, she picked up a little bit of stick, and held it out to the puppy; whereupon the puppy jumped into the air off all its feet at once, with a yelp of delight, and rushed at the stick, and made believe to worry it; then Alice dodged behind a great thistle, to keep herself from being run over; and the moment she appeared on the other side, the puppy made another rush at the stick, and tumbled head over heels in its hurry to get hold of it; then Alice, thinking it was very like having a game of play with a cart-horse, and expecting every moment to be trampled under its feet, ran round the thistle again; then the puppy began a series of short charges at the stick, running a very little way forwards each time and a long way back, and barking hoarsely all the while, till at last it sat down a good way off, panting, with its tongue hanging out of its mouth, and its great eyes half shut.

This seemed to Alice a good opportunity for making her escape; so she set off at once, and ran till she was quite tired and out of breath, and till the puppy's bark sounded quite faint in the distance.

'And yet what a dear little puppy it was!' said Alice, as

she leant against a buttercup to rest herself, and fanned herself with one of the leaves: 'I should have liked teaching it tricks very much, if—if I'd only been the right size to do it! Oh dear! I'd nearly forgotten that I've got to grow up again! Let me see—how *is* it to be managed? I suppose I ought to eat or drink something or other; but the great question is, what?'

The great question certainly was, what? Alice looked all round her at the flowers and the blades of grass, but she did not see anything that looked like the right thing to eat or drink under the circumstances. There was a large mushroom growing near her, about the same height as herself; and when she had looked under it, and on both sides of it, and behind it, it occurred to her that she might as well look and see what was on the top of it.

She stretched herself up on tiptoe, and peeped over the edge of the mushroom, and her eyes immediately met those of a large caterpillar, that was sitting on the top with its arms folded, quietly smoking a long hookah, and taking not the smallest notice of her or of anything else.

tiptoe ['tɪpˌto] *n* 腳趾尖；腳尖
caterpillar ['kætəˌpɪlə-] *n* 毛蟲

05 /

Advice from a Caterpillar

The Caterpillar and Alice looked at each other for some time in silence: at last the Caterpillar took the hookah out of its mouth, and addressed her in a languid, sleepy voice.

'Who are *you*?' said the Caterpillar.

This was not an encouraging opening for a conversation.

languid [ˈlæŋgwɪd] *adj* 不感興趣的，沒精打采的

Alice replied, rather shyly, 'I—I hardly know, sir, just at present—at least I know who I *was* when I got up this morning, but I think I must have been changed several times since then.'

'What do you mean by that?' said the Caterpillar sternly. 'Explain yourself!'

'I can't explain *myself*, I'm afraid, sir' said Alice, 'because I'm not myself, you see.'

'I don't see,' said the Caterpillar.

'I'm afraid I can't put it more clearly,' Alice replied very politely, 'for I can't understand it myself to begin with; and being so many different sizes in a day is very confusing.'

'It isn't,' said the Caterpillar.

'Well, perhaps you haven't found it so yet,' said Alice; 'but when you have to turn into a chrysalis—you will some day, you know—and then after that into a butterfly, I should think you'll feel it a little queer, won't you?'

'Not a bit,' said the Caterpillar.

'Well, perhaps your feelings may be different,' said Alice; 'all I know is, it would feel very queer to *me*.'

chrysalis ['krɪsəlɪs] *n* 【昆】蝶蛹：蟲繭

'You!' said the Caterpillar contemptuously. 'Who are *you?*'

Which brought them back again to the beginning of the conversation. Alice felt a little irritated at the Caterpillar's making such *very* short remarks, and she drew herself up and said, very gravely, 'I think, you ought to tell me who *you* are, first.'

'Why?' said the Caterpillar.

Here was another puzzling question; and as Alice could not think of any good reason, and as the Caterpillar seemed to be in a *very* unpleasant state of mind, she turned away.

'Come back!' the Caterpillar called after her. 'I've something important to say!'

This sounded promising, certainly: Alice turned and came back again.

'Keep your temper,' said the Caterpillar.

'Is that all?' said Alice, swallowing down her anger as well as she could.

'No,' said the Caterpillar.

Alice thought she might as well wait, as she had

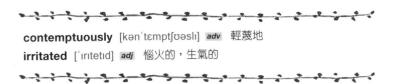

contemptuously [kənˈtɛmptʃʊəslɪ] *adv* 輕蔑地
irritated [ˈɪrɪtetɪd] *adj* 惱火的，生氣的

nothing else to do, and perhaps after all it might tell her something worth hearing. For some minutes it puffed away without speaking, but at last it unfolded its arms, took the hookah out of its mouth again, and said, 'So you think you're changed, do you?'

'I'm afraid I am, sir,' said Alice; 'I can't remember things as I used—and I don't keep the same size for ten minutes together!'

'Can't remember *what* things?' said the Caterpillar.

'Well, I've tried to say "How doth the little busy bee," but it all came different!' Alice replied in a very melancholy voice.

'Repeat, "*You are old, Father William,*"' said the Caterpillar.

Alice folded her hands, and began:—
'You are old, Father William,' the young man said,
'And your hair has become very white;
And yet you incessantly stand on your head—
Do you think, at your age, it is right?'

'In my youth,' Father William replied to his son,
'I feared it might injure the brain;

incessantly [ɪnˈsɛsntlɪ] *adv* 不斷地，不停地

But, now that I'm perfectly sure I have none,
Why, I do it again and again.'

'You are old,' said the youth, 'as I mentioned before,
And have grown most uncommonly fat;
Yet you turned a back-somersault in at the door—
Pray, what is the reason of that?'

'In my youth,' said the sage, as he shook his grey locks,

sage [sedʒ] *n* 賢人：哲人，德高望重的人

'I kept all my limbs very supple
By the use of this ointment—one shilling the box—
Allow me to sell you a couple?'

'You are old,' said the youth, 'and your jaws are too weak
For anything tougher than suet;
Yet you finished the goose, with the bones and the beak—

supple [ˈsʌpl] *adj* 易彎曲的，柔軟的
shilling [ˈʃɪlɪŋ] *n* 先令（1971 年前的英國貨幣單位，等於 12 便士，1 英鎊等於 20 先令）

Pray how did you manage to do it?'

'In my youth,' said his father, 'I took to the law,
And argued each case with my wife;
And the muscular strength, which it gave to my jaw,
Has lasted the rest of my life.'

'You are old,' said the youth, 'one would hardly suppose
That your eye was as steady as ever;
Yet you balanced an eel on the end of your nose—
What made you so awfully clever?'

'I have answered three questions, and that is enough,'

Said his father; 'don't give yourself airs!
Do you think I can listen all day to such stuff?
Be off, or I'll kick you down stairs!'

'That is not said right,' said the Caterpillar.

'Not *quite* right, I'm afraid,' said Alice, timidly; 'some of the words have got altered.'

'It is wrong from beginning to end,' said the Caterpillar decidedly, and there was silence for some minutes.

The Caterpillar was the first to speak.

'What size do you want to be?' it asked.

'Oh, I'm not particular as to size,' Alice hastily replied; 'only one doesn't like changing so often, you know.'

'I *don't* know,' said the Caterpillar.

Alice said nothing: she had never been so much contradicted in her life before, and she felt that she was losing her temper.

'Are you content now?' said the Caterpillar.

'Well, I should like to be a *little* larger, sir, if you wouldn't mind,' said Alice: 'three inches is such a wretched height to be.'

'It is a very good height indeed!' said the Caterpillar angrily, rearing itself upright as it spoke (it was exactly three inches high).

'But I'm not used to it!' pleaded poor Alice in a piteous tone. And she thought of herself, 'I wish the creatures wouldn't be so easily offended!'

'You'll get used to it in time,' said the Caterpillar; and it put the hookah into its mouth and began smoking again.

This time Alice waited patiently until it chose to speak again. In a minute or two the Caterpillar took the hookah out of its mouth and yawned once or twice, and shook itself. Then it got down off the mushroom, and crawled away in the grass, merely remarking as it went, 'One side will make you grow taller, and the other side will make you grow shorter.'

'One side of *what*? The other side of *what*?' thought Alice to herself.

'Of the mushroom,' said the Caterpillar, just as if she

had asked it aloud; and in another moment it was out of sight.

Alice remained looking thoughtfully at the mushroom for a minute, trying to make out which were the two sides of it; and as it was perfectly round, she found this a very difficult question. However, at last she stretched her arms round it as far as they would go, and broke off a bit of the edge with each hand.

'And now which is which?' she said to herself, and nibbled a little of the right-hand bit to try the effect: the next moment she felt a violent blow underneath her chin: it had struck her foot!

She was a good deal frightened by this very sudden change, but she felt that there was no time to be lost, as she was shrinking rapidly; so she set to work at once to eat some of the other bit. Her chin was pressed so closely against her foot, that there was hardly room to open her mouth; but she did it at last, and managed to swallow a morsel of the lefthand bit.

'Come, my head's free at last!' said Alice in a tone of delight, which changed into alarm in another moment, when she found that her shoulders were nowhere to be found: all she could see, when she looked down, was an

immense length of neck, which seemed to rise like a stalk out of a sea of green leaves that lay far below her.

'What *can* all that green stuff be?' said Alice. 'And where *have* my shoulders got to? And oh, my poor hands, how is it I can't see you?' She was moving them about as she spoke, but no result seemed to follow, except a little shaking among the distant green leaves.

As there seemed to be no chance of getting her hands up to her head, she tried to get her head down to them, and was delighted to find that her neck would bend about easily in any direction, like a serpent. She had just succeeded in curving it down into a graceful zigzag, and was going to dive in among the leaves, which she found to be nothing but the tops of the trees under which she had been wandering, when a sharp hiss made her draw back in a hurry: a large pigeon had flown into her face, and was beating her violently with its wings.

'Serpent!' screamed the Pigeon.

'I'm *not* a serpent!' said Alice indignantly. 'Let me alone!'

'Serpent, I say again!' repeated the Pigeon, but in a more subdued tone, and added with a kind of sob, 'I've

zigzag [ˈzɪgzæg] *n* 之字形的線條（或道路）；曲曲折折

sob [sɑb] *n* 嗚咽（聲），啜泣（聲）

tried every way, and nothing seems to suit them!'

'I haven't the least idea what you're talking about,' said Alice.

'I've tried the roots of trees, and I've tried banks, and I've tried hedges,' the Pigeon went on, without attending to her; 'but those serpents! There's no pleasing them!'

Alice was more and more puzzled, but she thought there was no use in saying anything more till the Pigeon had finished.

'As if it wasn't trouble enough hatching the eggs,' said the Pigeon; 'but I must be on the look-out for serpents night and day! Why, I haven't had a wink of sleep these three weeks!'

'I'm very sorry you've been annoyed,' said Alice, who was beginning to see its meaning.

'And just as I'd taken the highest tree in the wood,' continued the Pigeon, raising its voice to a shriek, 'and just as I was thinking I should be free of them at last, they must needs come wriggling down from the sky! Ugh, Serpent!'

'But I'm *not* a serpent, I tell you!' said Alice. 'I'm a— I'm a—'

'Well! *What* are you?' said the Pigeon. 'I can see you're trying to invent something!'

'I—I'm a little girl,' said Alice, rather doubtfully, as she remembered the number of changes she had gone

through that day.

'A likely story indeed!' said the Pigeon in a tone of the deepest contempt. 'I've seen a good many little girls in my time, but never *one* with such a neck as that! No, no! You're a serpent; and there's no use denying it. I suppose you'll be telling me next that you never tasted an egg!'

'I *have* tasted eggs, certainly,' said Alice, who was a very truthful child; 'but little girls eat eggs quite as much as serpents do, you know.'

'I don't believe it,' said the Pigeon; 'but if they do, why then they're a kind of serpent, that's all I can say.'

This was such a new idea to Alice, that she was quite silent for a minute or two, which gave the Pigeon the opportunity of adding, 'You're looking for eggs, I know *that* well enough; and what does it matter to me whether you're a little girl or a serpent?'

'It matters a good deal to *me*,' said Alice hastily; 'but I'm not looking for eggs, as it happens; and if I was, I shouldn't want *yours*: I don't like them raw.'

'Well, be off, then!' said the Pigeon in a sulky tone, as it settled down again into its nest. Alice crouched down among the trees as well as she could, for her neck kept

sulky [ˈsʌlkɪ] *adj* 生氣的，繃著臉的

getting entangled among the branches, and every now and then she had to stop and untwist it. After a while she remembered that she still held the pieces of mushroom in her hands, and she set to work very carefully, nibbling first at one and then at the other, and growing sometimes taller and sometimes shorter, until she had succeeded in bringing herself down to her usual height.

It was so long since she had been anything near the right size, that it felt quite strange at first; but she got used to it in a few minutes, and began talking to herself, as usual. 'Come, there's half my plan done now! How puzzling all these changes are! I'm never sure what I'm going to be, from one minute to another! However, I've got back to my right size: the next thing is, to get into that beautiful garden—how *is* that to be done, I wonder?' As she said this, she came suddenly upon an open place, with a little house in it about four feet high. 'Whoever lives there,' thought Alice, 'it'll never do to come upon them *this* size: why, I should frighten them out of their wits!' So she began nibbling at the righthand bit again, and did not venture to go near the house till she had brought herself down to nine inches high.

Pig and Pepper

For a minute or two she stood looking at the house,
and wondering what to do next, when suddenly a footman

in livery came running out of the wood—(she considered him to be a footman because he was in livery: otherwise, judging by his face only, she would have called him a fish)—and rapped loudly at the door with his knuckles. It was opened by another footman in livery, with a round face, and large eyes like a frog; and both footmen, Alice noticed, had powdered hair that curled all over their heads. She felt very curious to know what it was all about, and crept a little way out of the wood to listen.

The Fish-Footman began by producing from under his arm a great letter, nearly as large as himself, and this he handed over to the other, saying, in a solemn tone, 'For the Duchess. An invitation from the Queen to play croquet.' The Frog-Footman repeated, in the same solemn tone, only changing the order of the words a little, 'From the Queen. An invitation for the Duchess to play croquet.'

Then they both bowed low, and their curls got entangled together.

Alice laughed so much at this, that she had to run back into the wood for fear of their hearing her; and when she next peeped out the Fish-Footman was gone, and the other was sitting on the ground near the door,

livery [ˈlɪvərɪ] *n* （男僕等穿的或行業等採用的）制服

staring stupidly up into the sky.

Alice went timidly up to the door, and knocked.

'There's no sort of use in knocking,' said the Footman, 'and that for two reasons. First, because I'm on the same side of the door as you are; secondly, because they're making such a noise inside, no one could possibly hear you.' And certainly there *was* a most extraordinary noise going on within—a constant howling and sneezing, and every now and then a great crash, as if a dish or kettle had been broken to pieces.

'Please, then,' said Alice, 'how am I to get in?'

'There might be some sense in your knocking,' the Footman went on without attending to her, 'if we had the door between us. For instance, if you were *inside*, you might knock, and I could let you out, you know.' He was looking up into the sky all the time he was speaking, and this Alice thought decidedly uncivil. 'But perhaps he can't help it,' she said to herself; 'his eyes are so *very* nearly at the top of his head. But at any rate he might answer questions.—How am I to get in?' she repeated, aloud.

'I shall sit here,' the Footman remarked, 'till tomorrow—'

uncivil [ʌnˈsɪvl] *adj* 無禮的；失禮的

At this moment the door of the house opened, and a large plate came skimming out, straight at the Footman's head: it just grazed his nose, and broke to pieces against one of the trees behind him.

'—or next day, maybe,' the Footman continued in the same tone, exactly as if nothing had happened.

'How am I to get in?' asked Alice again, in a louder tone.

'*Are* you to get in at all?' said the Footman. 'That's the first question, you know.'

It was, no doubt: only Alice did not like to be told so. 'It's really dreadful,' she muttered to herself, 'the way all the creatures argue. It's enough to drive one crazy!'

The Footman seemed to think this a good opportunity for repeating his remark, with variations. 'I shall sit here,' he said, 'on and off, for days and days.'

'But what am *I* to do?' said Alice.

'Anything you like,' said the Footman, and began whistling.

'Oh, there's no use in talking to him,' said Alice desperately: 'he's perfectly idiotic!' And she opened the door and went in.

graze [grez] **v** 擦過，掠過

The door led right into a large kitchen, which was full of smoke from one end to the other: the Duchess was sitting on a three-legged stool in the middle, nursing a baby; the cook was leaning over the fire, stirring a large cauldron which seemed to be full of soup.

'There's certainly too much pepper in that soup!' Alice said to herself, as well as she could for sneezing.

cauldron ['kɔldrən] *n* 大鍋；大汽鍋

There was certainly too much of it in the air. Even the Duchess sneezed occasionally; and as for the baby, it was sneezing and howling alternately without a moment's pause. The only things in the kitchen that did not sneeze, were the cook, and a large cat which was sitting on the hearth and grinning from ear to ear.

'Please would you tell me,' said Alice, a little timidly, for she was not quite sure whether it was good manners for her to speak first, 'why your cat grins like that?'

'It's a Cheshire cat,' said the Duchess, 'and that's why. Pig!'

She said the last word with such sudden violence that Alice quite jumped; but she saw in another moment that it was addressed to the baby, and not to her, so she took courage, and went on again:—

'I didn't know that Cheshire cats always grinned; in fact, I didn't know that cats *could* grin.'

'They all can,' said the Duchess; 'and most of 'em do.'

'I don't know of any that do,' Alice said very politely, feeling quite pleased to have got into a conversation.

'You don't know much,' said the Duchess; 'and that's a fact.'

Alice did not at all like the tone of this remark, and thought it would be as well to introduce some other subject of conversation. While she was trying to fix on one, the cook took the cauldron of soup off the fire, and

at once set to work throwing everything within her reach at the Duchess and the baby—the fire-irons came first; then followed a shower of saucepans, plates, and dishes. The Duchess took no notice of them even when they hit her; and the baby was howling so much already, that it was quite impossible to say whether the blows hurt it or not.

'Oh, *please* mind what you're doing!' cried Alice, jumping up and down in an agony of terror. 'Oh, there goes his *precious* nose'; as an unusually large saucepan flew close by it, and very nearly carried it off.

'If everybody minded their own business,' the Duchess said in a hoarse growl, 'the world would go round a deal faster than it does.'

'Which would *not* be an advantage,' said Alice, who felt very glad to get an opportunity of showing off a little of her knowledge. 'Just think of what work it would make with the day and night! You see the earth takes twenty-four hours to turn round on its axis—'

'Talking of axes,' said the Duchess, 'chop off her head!'

Alice glanced rather anxiously at the cook, to see if she meant to take the hint; but the cook was busily stirring the soup, and seemed not to be listening, so she went on again: 'Twenty-four hours, I *think*; or is it twelve? I—'

'Oh, don't bother *me*,' said the Duchess; 'I never could abide figures!' And with that she began nursing her

child again, singing a sort of lullaby to it as she did so, and giving it a violent shake at the end of every line:

'Speak roughly to your little boy,
And beat him when he sneezes:
He only does it to annoy,
Because he knows it teases.'

CHORUS.
(In which the cook and the baby joined):—

'Wow! wow! wow!'

While the Duchess sang the second verse of the song, she kept tossing the baby violently up and down, and the poor little thing howled so, that Alice could hardly hear the words:—

'I speak severely to my boy,
I beat him when he sneezes;
For he can thoroughly enjoy
The pepper when he pleases!'

CHORUS.

'Wow! wow! wow!'

tease [tiz] *v* 戲弄，逗弄

'Here! you may nurse it a bit, if you like!' the Duchess said to Alice, flinging the baby at her as she spoke. 'I must go and get ready to play croquet with the Queen,' and she hurried out of the room. The cook threw a frying-pan after her as she went out, but it just missed her.

Alice caught the baby with some difficulty, as it was a queer-shaped little creature, and held out its arms and legs in all directions, 'just like a star-fish,' thought Alice. The poor little thing was snorting like a steam-engine when she caught it, and kept doubling itself up and straightening itself out again, so that altogether, for the first minute or two, it was as much as she could do to hold it.

As soon as she had made out the proper way of nursing it, (which was to twist it up into a sort of knot, and then keep tight hold of its right ear and left foot, so as to prevent its undoing itself,) she carried it out into the open air. 'If I don't take this child away with me,' thought Alice, 'they're sure to kill it in a day or two: wouldn't it be murder to leave it behind?' She said the last words out loud, and the little thing grunted in reply (it had left off sneezing by this time). 'Don't grunt,' said Alice; 'that's not at all a proper way of expressing yourself.'

The baby grunted again, and Alice looked very anxiously into its face to see what was the matter with it. There could be no doubt that it had a *very* turn-up nose,

much more like a snout than a real nose; also its eyes were getting extremely small for a baby: altogether Alice did not like the look of the thing at all. 'But perhaps it was only sobbing,' she thought, and looked into its eyes again, to see if there were any tears.

No, there were no tears. 'If you're going to turn into a pig, my dear,' said Alice, seriously, 'I'll have nothing more to do with you. Mind now!' The poor little thing sobbed again (or grunted, it was impossible to say which), and they went on for some while in silence.

Alice was just beginning to think to herself, 'Now, what am I to do with this creature when I get it home?' when it grunted again, so violently, that she looked down into its face in

snout [snaʊt] *n* （動物的）口鼻部位；豬嘴

some alarm. This time there could be *no* mistake about it: it was neither more nor less than a pig, and she felt that it would be quite absurd for her to carry it further.

So she set the little creature down, and felt quite relieved to see it trot away quietly into the wood. 'If it had grown up,' she said to herself, 'it would have made a dreadfully ugly child: but it makes rather a handsome pig, I think.' And she began thinking over other children she knew, who might do very well as pigs, and was just saying to herself, 'if one only knew the right way to change them—' when she was a little startled by seeing the Cheshire Cat sitting on a bough of a tree a few yards off.

The Cat only grinned when it saw Alice. It looked good-natured, she thought: still it had *very* long claws and a great many teeth, so she felt that it ought to be treated with respect.

'Cheshire Puss,' she began, rather timidly, as she did not at all know whether it would like the name: however, it only grinned a little wider. 'Come, it's pleased so far,' thought Alice, and she went on. 'Would you tell me, please, which way I ought to go from here?'

'That depends a good deal on where you want to get to,' said the Cat.

'I don't much care where—' said Alice.

'Then it doesn't matter which way you go,' said the Cat.

'—so long as I get
somewhere,' Alice added as
an explanation.

'Oh, you're sure to do
that,' said the Cat, 'if you
only walk long enough.'

Alice felt that this
could not be denied, so
she tried another question.
'What sort of people live
about here?'

'In *that* direction,' the
Cat said, waving its right

paw round, 'lives a Hatter: and in *that* direction,' waving the other paw, 'lives a March Hare. Visit either you like: they're both mad.'

'But I don't want to go among mad people,' Alice remarked.

'Oh, you can't help that,' said the Cat: 'we're all mad here. I'm mad. You're mad.'

'How do you know I'm mad?' said Alice.

'You must be,' said the Cat, 'or you wouldn't have come here.'

Alice didn't think that proved it at all; however, she went on 'And how do you know that you're mad?'

'To begin with,' said the Cat, 'a dog's not mad. You grant that?'

'I suppose so,' said Alice.

'Well, then,' the Cat went on, 'you see, a dog growls when it's angry, and wags its tail when it's pleased. Now *I* growl when I'm pleased, and wag my tail when I'm angry. Therefore I'm mad.'

'*I* call it purring, not growling,' said Alice.

'Call it what you like,' said the Cat. 'Do you play croquet with the Queen to-day?'

hatter ['hætə] *n* 帽匠

'I should like it very much,' said Alice, 'but I haven't been invited yet.'

'You'll see me there,' said the Cat, and vanished.

Alice was not much surprised at this, she was getting so used to queer things happening. While she was looking at the place where it had been, it suddenly appeared again.

'By-the-bye, what became of the baby?' said the Cat. 'I'd nearly forgotten to ask.'

'It turned into a pig,' Alice quietly said, just as if it had come back in a natural way.

'I thought it would,' said the Cat, and vanished again.

Alice waited a little, half expecting to see it again, but it did not appear, and after a minute or two she walked on in the direction in which the March Hare was said to live. 'I've seen hatters before,' she said to herself; 'the March Hare will be much the most interesting, and perhaps as this is May it won't be raving mad—at least not so mad as it was in March.' As she said this, she looked up, and there was the Cat again, sitting on a branch of a tree.

'Did you say pig, or fig?' said the Cat.

'I said pig,' replied Alice; 'and I wish you wouldn't keep appearing and vanishing so suddenly: you make one quite giddy.'

'All right,' said the Cat; and this time it vanished quite slowly, beginning with the end of the tail, and ending with the grin, which remained some time after the rest of it

had gone.

'Well! I've often seen a cat without a grin,' thought Alice; 'but a grin without a cat! It's the most curious thing I ever saw in my life!'

She had not gone much farther before she came in sight of the house of the March Hare: she thought it must be the right house, because the chimneys were shaped like ears and the roof was thatched with fur. It was so large a house, that she did not like to go nearer till she had nibbled some more of the lefthand bit of mushroom, and raised herself to about two feet high: even then she walked up towards it rather timidly, saying to herself 'Suppose it should be raving mad after all! I almost wish I'd gone to see the Hatter instead!'

07 /

A Mad Tea-Party

There was a table set out under a tree in front of the house, and the March Hare and the Hatter were having tea at it: a Dormouse was sitting between them, fast asleep, and the other two were using it as a cushion, resting their

elbows on it, and talking over its head. 'Very uncomfortable for the Dormouse,' thought Alice; 'only, as it's asleep, I suppose it doesn't mind.'

The table was a large one, but the three were all crowded together at one corner of it: 'No room! No room!' they cried out when they saw Alice coming. 'There's *plenty* of room!' said Alice indignantly, and she sat down in a large arm-chair at one end of the table.

'Have some wine,' the March Hare said in an encouraging tone.

Alice looked all round the table, but there was nothing on it but tea. 'I don't see any wine,' she remarked.

'There isn't any,' said the March Hare.

'Then it wasn't very civil of you to offer it,' said Alice angrily.

'It wasn't very civil of you to sit down without being invited,' said the March Hare.

'I didn't know it was *your* table,' said Alice; 'it's laid for a great many more than three.'

'Your hair wants cutting,' said the Hatter. He had been looking at Alice for some time with great curiosity, and this was his first speech.

'You should learn not to make personal remarks,'

Alice said with some severity; 'it's very rude.'

The Hatter opened his eyes very wide on hearing this; but all he *said* was, 'Why is a raven like a writing-desk?'

'Come, we shall have some fun now!' thought Alice. 'I'm glad they've begun asking riddles.—I believe I can guess that,' she added aloud.

'Do you mean that you think you can find out the answer to it?' said the March Hare.

'Exactly so,' said Alice.

'Then you should say what you mean,' the March Hare went on.

'I do,' Alice hastily replied; 'at least—at least I mean what I say—that's the same thing, you know.'

'Not the same thing a bit!' said the Hatter. 'You might just as well say that "I see what I eat" is the same thing as "I eat what I see"!'

'You might just as well say,' added the March Hare, 'that "I like what I get" is the same thing as "I get what I like"!'

'You might just as well say,' added the Dormouse, who seemed to be talking in his sleep, 'that "I breathe

severity [səˈvɛrətɪ] *n* 嚴厲；嚴肅
riddle [ˈrɪdl] *n* 謎語

when I sleep" is the same thing as "I sleep when I breathe"!'

'It *is* the same thing with you,' said the Hatter, and here the conversation dropped, and the party sat silent for a minute, while Alice thought over all she could remember about ravens and writing-desks, which wasn't much.

The Hatter was the first to break the silence. 'What day of the month is it?' he said, turning to Alice: he had taken his watch out of his pocket, and was looking at it uneasily, shaking it every now and then, and holding it to his ear.

Alice considered a little, and then said 'The fourth.'

'Two days wrong!' sighed the Hatter. 'I told you butter wouldn't suit the works!' he added looking angrily at the March Hare.

'It was the *best* butter,' the March Hare meekly replied.

'Yes, but some crumbs must have got in as well,' the Hatter grumbled: 'you shouldn't have put it in with the bread-knife.'

The March Hare took the watch and looked at it gloomily: then he dipped it into his cup of tea, and looked at it again: but he could think of nothing better to say

meekly [ˈmiklɪ] *adv* 溫順地；逆來順受地

than his first remark, 'It was the *best* butter, you know.'

Alice had been looking over his shoulder with some curiosity. 'What a funny watch!' she remarked. 'It tells the day of the month, and doesn't tell what o'clock it is!'

'Why should it?' muttered the Hatter. 'Does *your* watch tell you what year it is?'

'Of course not,' Alice replied very readily: 'but that's because it stays the same year for such a long time together.'

'Which is just the case with *mine*,' said the Hatter.

Alice felt dreadfully puzzled. The Hatter's remark seemed to have no sort of meaning in it, and yet it was certainly English. 'I don't quite understand you,' she said, as politely as she could.

'The Dormouse is asleep again,' said the Hatter, and he poured a little hot tea upon its nose.

The Dormouse shook its head impatiently, and said, without opening its eyes, 'Of course, of course; just what I was going to remark myself.'

'Have you guessed the riddle yet?' the Hatter said, turning to Alice again.

'No, I give it up,' Alice replied: 'what's the answer?'

'I haven't the slightest idea,' said the Hatter.

'Nor I,' said the March Hare.

Alice sighed wearily. 'I think you might do something better with the time,' she said, 'than waste it in asking

riddles that have no answers.'

'If you knew Time as well as I do,' said the Hatter, 'you wouldn't talk about wasting *it*. It's *him*.'

'I don't know what you mean,' said Alice.

'Of course you don't!' the Hatter said, tossing his head contemptuously. 'I dare say you never even spoke to Time!'

'Perhaps not,' Alice cautiously replied: 'but I know I have to beat time when I learn music.'

'Ah! that accounts for it,' said the Hatter. 'He won't stand beating. Now, if you only kept on good terms with him, he'd do almost anything you liked with the clock. For instance, suppose it were nine o'clock in the morning, just time to begin lessons: you'd only have to whisper a hint to Time, and round goes the clock in a twinkling! Half-past one, time for dinner!'

('I only wish it was,' the March Hare said to itself in a whisper.)

'That would be grand, certainly,' said Alice thoughtfully:

'but then—I shouldn't be hungry for it, you know.'

'Not at first, perhaps,' said the Hatter: 'but you could keep it to half-past one as long as you liked.'

'Is that the way *you* manage?' Alice asked.

The Hatter shook his head mournfully. 'Not I!' he replied. 'We quarrelled last March—just before *he* went mad, you know—' (pointing with his tea spoon at the March Hare,) '—it was at the great concert given by the Queen of Hearts, and I had to sing

> *"Twinkle, twinkle, little bat!*
> *How I wonder what you're at!"*

You know the song, perhaps?'

'I've heard something like it,' said Alice.

'It goes on, you know,' the Hatter continued, 'in this way:—

> *"Up above the world you fly,*
> *Like a tea-tray in the sky.*
> *Twinkle, twinkle—"'*

Here the Dormouse shook itself, and began singing in its sleep '*Twinkle, twinkle, twinkle, twinkle—*' and went on so long that they had to pinch it to make it stop.

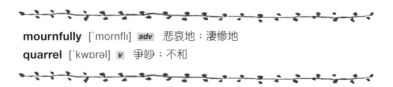

mournfully ['mɔrnflɪ] *adv* 悲哀地；淒慘地
quarrel ['kwɒrəl] *v* 爭吵；不和

'Well, I'd hardly finished the first verse,' said the Hatter, 'when the Queen jumped up and bawled out, "He's murdering the time! Off with his head!"'

'How dreadfully savage!' exclaimed Alice.

'And ever since that,' the Hatter went on in a mournful tone, 'he won't do a thing I ask! It's always six o'clock now.'

A bright idea came into Alice's head. 'Is that the reason so many tea-things are put out here?' she asked.

'Yes, that's it,' said the Hatter with a sigh: 'it's always tea-time, and we've no time to wash the things between whiles.'

'Then you keep moving round, I suppose?' said Alice.

'Exactly so,' said the Hatter: 'as the things get used up.'

'But what happens when you come to the beginning again?' Alice ventured to ask.

'Suppose we change the subject,' the March Hare interrupted, yawning. 'I'm getting tired of this. I vote the young lady tells us a story.'

'I'm afraid I don't know one,' said Alice, rather alarmed at the proposal.

'Then the Dormouse shall!' they both cried. 'Wake up, Dormouse!' And they pinched it on both sides at once.

The Dormouse slowly opened his eyes. 'I wasn't asleep,' he said in a hoarse, feeble voice: 'I heard every

word you fellows were saying.'

'Tell us a story!' said the March Hare.

'Yes, please do!' pleaded Alice.

'And be quick about it,' added the Hatter, 'or you'll be asleep again before it's done.'

'Once upon a time there were three little sisters,' the Dormouse began in a great hurry; 'and their names were Elsie, Lacie, and Tillie; and they lived at the bottom of a well—'

'What did they live on?' said Alice, who always took a great interest in questions of eating and drinking.

'They lived on treacle,' said the Dormouse, after thinking a minute or two.

'They couldn't have done that, you know,' Alice gently remarked; 'they'd have been ill.'

'So they were,' said the Dormouse; '*very* ill.'

Alice tried to fancy to herself what such an extraordinary ways of living would be like, but it puzzled her too much, so she went on: 'But why did they live at the bottom of a well?'

'Take some more tea,' the March Hare said to Alice, very earnestly.

treacle ['trikl] *n* 糖蜜

'I've had nothing yet,' Alice replied in an offended tone, 'so I can't take more.'

'You mean you can't take *less*,' said the Hatter: 'it's very easy to take *more* than nothing.'

'Nobody asked *your* opinion,' said Alice.

'Who's making personal remarks now?' the Hatter asked triumphantly.

Alice did not quite know what to say to this: so she helped herself to some tea and bread-and-butter, and then turned to the Dormouse, and repeated her question. 'Why did they live at the bottom of a well?'

The Dormouse again took a minute or two to think about it, and then said, 'It was a treacle-well.'

'There's no such thing!' Alice was beginning very angrily, but the Hatter and the March Hare went 'Sh! sh!' and the Dormouse sulkily remarked, 'If you can't be civil, you'd better finish the story for yourself.'

'No, please go on!' Alice said very humbly; 'I won't interrupt again. I dare say there may be *one*.'

'One, indeed!' said the Dormouse indignantly. However, he consented to go on. 'And so these three little sisters—they were learning to draw, you know—'

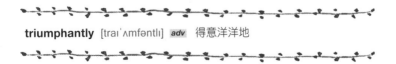

triumphantly [traɪˈʌmfəntlɪ] *adv* 得意洋洋地

'What did they draw?' said Alice, quite forgetting her promise.

'Treacle,' said the Dormouse, without considering at all this time.

'I want a clean cup,' interrupted the Hatter: 'let's all move one place on.'

He moved on as he spoke, and the Dormouse followed him: the March Hare moved into the Dormouse's place, and Alice rather unwillingly took the place of the March Hare. The Hatter was the only one who got any advantage from the change: and Alice was a good deal worse off than before, as the March Hare had just upset the milk-jug into his plate.

Alice did not wish to offend the Dormouse again, so she began very cautiously: 'But I don't understand. Where did they draw the treacle from?'

'You can draw water out of a water-well,' said the Hatter; 'so I should think you could draw treacle out of a treacle-well—eh, stupid?'

'But they were *in* the well,' Alice said to the Dormouse, not choosing to notice this last remark.

'Of course they were', said the Dormouse; '—well in.'

This answer so confused poor Alice, that she let the Dormouse go on for some time without interrupting it.

'They were learning to draw,' the Dormouse went on, yawning and rubbing its eyes, for it was getting very

sleepy; 'and they drew all manner of things—everything that begins with an M—'

'Why with an M?' said Alice.

'Why not?' said the March Hare.

Alice was silent.

The Dormouse had closed its eyes by this time, and was going off into a doze; but, on being pinched by the Hatter, it woke up again with a little shriek, and went on: '—that begins with an M, such as mouse-traps, and the moon, and memory, and muchness—you know you say things are "much of a muchness"—did you ever see such a thing as a drawing of a muchness?'

'Really, now you ask me,' said Alice, very much confused, 'I don't think—'

'Then you shouldn't talk,' said the Hatter.

This piece of rudeness was more than Alice could bear: she got up in great disgust, and walked off; the Dormouse fell asleep instantly, and neither of the others took the least notice of her going, though she looked back once or twice, half hoping that they would call after her: the last time she saw them, they were trying to put the Dormouse into the teapot.

'At any rate I'll never go *there* again!' said Alice as she picked her way through the wood. 'It's the stupidest tea-party I ever was at in all my life!'

Just as she said this, she noticed that one of the trees

had a door leading right into it. 'That's very curious!' she
thought. 'But everything's curious today. I think I may as
well go in at once.' And in she went.

Once more she found herself in the long hall, and
close to the little glass table. 'Now, I'll manage better this
time,' she said to herself, and began by taking the little
golden key, and unlocking the door that led into the
garden. Then she went to work nibbling at the mushroom
(she had kept a piece of it in her pocket) till she was about
a foot high: then she walked down the little passage: and
then—she found herself at last in the beautiful garden,
among the bright flower-beds and the cool fountains.

The Queen's Croquet-Ground

A large rose-tree stood near the entrance of the garden: the roses growing on it were white, but there were three gardeners at it, busily painting them red. Alice thought this a very curious thing, and she went nearer to

watch them, and just as she came up to them she heard one of them say, 'Look out now, Five! Don't go splashing paint over me like that!'

'I couldn't help it,' said Five, in a sulky tone; 'Seven jogged my elbow.'

On which Seven looked up and said, 'That's right, Five! Always lay the blame on others!'

'*You'd* better not talk!' said Five. 'I heard the Queen say only yesterday you deserved to be beheaded!'

'What for?' said the one who had spoken first.

'That's none of *your* business, Two!' said Seven.

'Yes, it *is* his business!' said Five, 'and I'll tell him—it was for bringing the cook tulip-roots instead of onions.'

Seven flung down his brush, and had just begun 'Well, of all the unjust things—' when his eye chanced to fall upon Alice, as she stood watching them, and he checked himself suddenly: the others looked round also, and all of them bowed low.

'Would you tell me,' said Alice, a little timidly, 'why you are painting those roses?'

Five and Seven said nothing, but looked at Two. Two began in a low voice, 'Why the fact is, you see, Miss, this here ought to have been a *red* rose-tree, and we put a white one in by mistake; and if the Queen was to find it out, we should all have our heads cut off, you know. So you see, Miss, we're doing our best, afore she comes, to—'

At this moment Five, who had been anxiously looking across the garden, called out 'The Queen! The Queen!' and the three gardeners instantly threw themselves flat upon their faces. There was a sound of many footsteps, and Alice looked round, eager to see the Queen.

First came ten soldiers carrying clubs; these were all shaped like the three gardeners, oblong and flat, with their hands and feet at the corners: next the ten courtiers; these were ornamented all over with diamonds, and walked two and two, as the soldiers did. After these came the royal children; there were ten of them, and the little dears came jumping merrily along hand in hand, in couples: they were all ornamented with hearts. Next came the guests, mostly Kings and Queens, and among them Alice recognised the White Rabbit: it was talking in a hurried nervous manner, smiling at everything that was said, and went by without noticing her. Then followed the Knave of Hearts, carrying the King's crown on a crimson velvet cushion; and, last of all this grand procession, came THE KING AND

courtier ['kortjə-] *n* 廷臣，朝臣
ornament ['ɔrnəmənt] *v* 裝飾
knave [nev] *n* （紙牌中的）傑克
crimson ['krɪmzn̩] *adj* 深紅色的，緋紅的

QUEEN OF HEARTS.

Alice was rather doubtful whether she ought not to lie down on her face like the three gardeners, but she could not remember ever having heard of such a rule at processions; 'and besides, what would be the use of a procession,' thought she, 'if people had all to lie down upon their faces, so that they couldn't see it?' So she stood still where she was, and waited.

When the procession came opposite to Alice, they all stopped and looked at her, and the Queen said severely 'Who is this?' She said it to the Knave of Hearts, who only bowed and smiled in reply.

'Idiot!' said the Queen, tossing her head impatiently; and, turning to Alice, she went on, 'What's your name, child?'

'My name is Alice, so please your Majesty,' said Alice very politely; but she added, to herself, 'Why, they're only a pack of cards, after all. I needn't be afraid of them!'

'And who are *these*?' said the Queen, pointing to the three gardeners who were lying round the rosetree; for, you see, as they were lying on their faces, and the pattern on their backs was the same as the rest of the pack, she could not tell whether they were gardeners, or soldiers, or courtiers, or three of her own children.

'How should *I* know?' said Alice, surprised at her own courage. 'It's no business of *mine*.'

The Queen turned crimson with fury, and, after glaring at her for a moment like a wild beast, screamed 'Off with her head! Off—'

'Nonsense!' said Alice, very loudly and decidedly, and the Queen was silent.

The King laid his hand upon her arm, and timidly said 'Consider, my dear: she is only a child!'

The Queen turned angrily away from him, and said to the Knave 'Turn them over!'

The Knave did so, very carefully, with one foot.

'Get up!' said the Queen, in a shrill, loud voice, and the three gardeners instantly jumped up, and began bowing to the King, the Queen, the royal children, and everybody else.

'Leave off that!' screamed the Queen. 'You make me giddy.' And then, turning to the rose-tree, she went on, 'What *have* you been doing here?'

'May it please your Majesty,' said Two, in a very humble tone, going down on one knee as he spoke, 'we were trying—'

'*I* see!' said the Queen, who had meanwhile been examining the roses. 'Off with their heads!' and the procession moved on, three of the soldiers remaining behind to execute the unfortunate gardeners, who ran to Alice for protection.

'You shan't be beheaded!' said Alice, and she put them into a large flower-pot that stood near. The three soldiers wandered about for a minute or two, looking for them, and then quietly marched off after the others.

'Are their heads off?' shouted the Queen.

'Their heads are gone, if it please your Majesty!' the soldiers shouted in reply.

'That's right!' shouted the Queen. 'Can you play croquet?'

The soldiers were silent, and looked at Alice, as the question was evidently meant for her.

'Yes!' shouted Alice.

'Come on, then!' roared the Queen, and Alice joined the procession, wondering very much what would happen next.

'It's—it's a very fine day!' said a timid voice at her side. She was walking by the White Rabbit, who was peeping anxiously into her face.

'Very,' said Alice: '—where's the Duchess?'

'Hush! Hush!' said the Rabbit in a low, hurried tone. He looked anxiously over his shoulder as he spoke, and then raised himself upon tiptoe, put his mouth close to her ear, and whispered 'She's under sentence of execution.'

'What for?' said Alice.

'Did you say "What a pity!"?' the Rabbit asked.

execution [ˌɛksɪˈkjuʃən] *n* 死刑

'No, I didn't,' said Alice: 'I don't think it's at all a pity. I said "What for?"'

'She boxed the Queen's ears—' the Rabbit began. Alice gave a little scream of laughter. 'Oh, hush!' the Rabbit whispered in a frightened tone. 'The Queen will hear you! You see, she came rather late, and the Queen said—'

'Get to your places!' shouted the Queen in a voice of thunder, and people began running about in all directions, tumbling up against each other; however, they got settled down in a minute or two, and the game began. Alice thought she had never seen such a curious croquet-ground in her life; it was all ridges and furrows; the balls were live hedgehogs, the mallets live flamingoes, and the soldiers had to double themselves up and to stand on their hands and feet, to make the arches.

The chief difficulty Alice found at first was in managing her flamingo: she succeeded in getting its body tucked away, comfortably enough, under her arm, with its

hedgehog [ˈhɛdʒˌhɑg] *n* 刺蝟
mallet [ˈmælɪt] *n* 球棍；槌球棒
flamingo [fləˈmɪŋgo] *n* 紅鶴
arch [ɑrtʃ] *n* 拱形物；拱形

legs hanging down, but generally, just as she had got its neck nicely straightened out, and was going to give the hedgehog a blow with its head, it *would* twist itself round and look up in her face, with such a puzzled expression that she could not help bursting out laughing: and when she had got its head down, and was going to begin again, it was very provoking to find that the hedgehog had unrolled itself, and was in the act of crawling away: besides all this, there was generally a ridge or furrow in the way wherever she wanted to send the hedgehog to, and, as the doubled-up soldiers were always getting up and walking off to other parts of the ground, Alice soon came to the conclusion that it was a very difficult game indeed.

The players all played at once without waiting for turns, quarrelling all the while, and fighting for the hedgehogs; and in a very short time the Queen was in a furious passion, and went stamping about, and shouting 'Off with his head!' or 'Off with her head!' about once in

a minute.

Alice began to feel very uneasy: to be sure, she had not as yet had any dispute with the Queen, but she knew that it might happen any minute, 'and then,' thought she, 'what would become of me? They're dreadfully fond of beheading people here; the great wonder is, that there's any one left alive!'

She was looking about for some way of escape, and wondering whether she could get away without being seen, when she noticed a curious appearance in the air: it puzzled her very much at first, but, after watching it a minute or two, she made it out to be a grin, and she said to herself 'It's the Cheshire Cat: now I shall have somebody to talk to.'

'How are you getting on?' said the Cat, as soon as there was mouth enough for it to speak with.

Alice waited till the eyes appeared, and then nodded. 'It's no use speaking to it,' she thought, 'till its ears have come, or at least one of them.' In another minute the whole head appeared, and then Alice put down her flamingo, and began an account of the game, feeling very glad she had someone to listen to her. The Cat seemed to

dispute [dɪˈspjut] *n* 爭論；爭執

think that there was enough of it now in sight, and no more of it appeared.

'I don't think they play at all fairly,' Alice began, in rather a complaining tone, 'and they all quarrel so dreadfully one can't hear oneself speak—and they don't seem to have any rules in particular; at least, if there are, nobody attends to them—and you've no idea how confusing it is all the things being alive; for instance, there's the arch I've got to go through next walking about at the other end of the ground—and I should have croqueted the Queen's hedgehog just now, only it ran away when it saw mine coming!'

'How do you like the Queen?' said the Cat in a low voice.

'Not at all,' said Alice: 'she's so extremely—' Just then she noticed that the Queen was close behind her, listening: so she went on, '—likely to win, that it's hardly worth while finishing the game.'

The Queen smiled and passed on.

'Who *are* you talking to?' said the King, going up to Alice, and looking at the Cat's head with great curiosity.

'It's a friend of mine—a Cheshire Cat,' said Alice: 'allow me to introduce it.'

'I don't like the look of it at all,' said the King: 'however, it may kiss my hand if it likes.'

'I'd rather not,' the Cat remarked.

'Don't be impertinent,' said the King, 'and don't look at me like that!' He got behind Alice as he spoke.

'A cat may look at a king,' said Alice. 'I've read that in some book, but I don't remember where.'

'Well, it must be removed,' said the King very decidedly, and he called the Queen, who was passing at the moment, 'My dear! I wish you would have this cat removed!'

The Queen had only one way of settling all difficulties, great or small. 'Off with his head!' she said, without even looking round.

'I'll fetch the executioner myself,' said the King eagerly, and he hurried off.

Alice thought she might as well go back, and see how the game was going on, as she heard the Queen's voice in the distance, screaming with passion. She had already heard her sentence three of the players to be executed for having missed their turns, and she did not like the look of things at all, as the game was in such confusion that she never knew whether it was her turn or not. So she went in search of her hedgehog.

The hedgehog was engaged in a fight with another

impertinent [ɪmˈpɜːtnənt] *adj* 無禮的；傲慢的

hedgehog, which seemed to Alice an excellent opportunity for croqueting one of them with the other: the only difficulty was, that her flamingo was gone across to the other side of the garden, where Alice could see it trying in a helpless sort of way to fly up into a tree.

By the time she had caught the flamingo and brought it back, the fight was over, and both the hedgehogs were out of sight: 'but it doesn't matter much,' thought Alice, 'as all the arches are gone from this side of the ground.' So she tucked it away under her arm, that it might not escape again, and went back for a little more conversation with her friend.

When she got back to the Cheshire Cat, she was surprised to find quite a large crowd collected round it: there was a dispute going on between the executioner, the King, and the Queen, who were all talking at once, while all the rest were quite silent, and looked very uncomfortable.

The moment Alice appeared, she was appealed to by all three to settle the question, and they repeated their arguments to her, though, as they all spoke at once, she found it very hard indeed to make out exactly what they said.

The executioner's argument was, that you couldn't cut off a head unless there was a body to cut it off from: that he had never had to do such a thing before, and he wasn't going to begin at *his* time of life.

The King's argument was, that anything that had a head could be beheaded, and that you weren't to talk nonsense.

The Queen's argument was, that if something wasn't done about it in less than no time she'd have everybody executed, all round. (It was this last remark that had made the whole party look so grave and anxious.)

Alice could think of nothing else to say but 'It belongs to the Duchess: you'd better ask *her* about it.'

'She's in prison,' the Queen said to the executioner: 'fetch her here.' And the executioner went off like an arrow.

The Cat's head began fading away the moment he was gone, and, by the time he had come back with the Duchess, it had entirely disappeared; so the King and the executioner ran wildly up and down looking for it, while the rest of the party went back to the game.

09 /

The Mock Turtle's Story

'You can't think how glad I am to see you again, you dear old thing!' said the Duchess, as she tucked her arm affectionately into Alice's, and they walked off together.

Alice was very glad to find her in such a pleasant temper, and thought to herself that perhaps it was only the pepper that had made her so savage when they met in the kitchen.

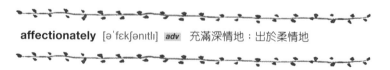

affectionately [əˈfɛkʃənɪtlɪ] *adv* 充滿深情地；出於柔情地

'When *I'm* a Duchess,' she said to herself, (not in a very hopeful tone though), 'I won't have any pepper in my kitchen *at all.* Soup does very well without—Maybe it's always pepper that makes people hot-tempered,' she went on, very much pleased at having found out a new kind of rule, 'and vinegar that makes them sour—and camomile that makes them bitter—and—and barley-sugar and such things that make children sweet-tempered. I only wish people knew *that*: then they wouldn't be so stingy about it, you know—'

She had quite forgotten the Duchess by this time, and was a little startled when she heard her voice close to her ear. 'You're thinking about something, my dear, and that makes you forget to talk. I can't tell you just now what the moral of that is, but I shall remember it in a bit.'

'Perhaps it hasn't one,' Alice ventured to remark.

'Tut, tut, child!' said the Duchess. 'Everything's got a moral, if only you can find it.' And she squeezed herself up closer to Alice's side as she spoke.

Alice did not much like keeping so close to her: first, because the Duchess was *very* ugly; and secondly, because she was exactly the right height to rest her chin upon Alice's shoulder, and it was an uncomfortably sharp chin. However, she did not like to be rude, so she bore it as well as she could.

'The game's going on rather better now,' she said, by

way of keeping up the conversation a little.

"'Tis so,' said the Duchess: 'and the moral of that is—"Oh, 'tis love, 'tis love, that makes the world go round!"'

'Somebody said,' Alice whispered, 'that it's done by everybody minding their own business!'

'Ah, well! It means much the same thing,' said the Duchess, digging her sharp little chin into Alice's shoulder as she added, 'and the moral of *that* is—"Take care of the sense, and the sounds will take care of themselves."'

'How fond she is of finding morals in things!' Alice thought to herself.

'I dare say you're wondering why I don't put my arm round your waist,' the Duchess said after a pause: 'the reason is, that I'm doubtful about the temper of your flamingo. Shall I try the experiment?'

'He might bite,' Alice cautiously replied, not feeling at all anxious to have the experiment tried.

'Very true,' said the Duchess: 'flamingoes and mustard both bite. And the moral of that is—"Birds of a feather flock together."'

'Only mustard isn't a bird,' Alice remarked.

'Right, as usual,' said the Duchess: 'what a clear way

moral [ˈmɒrəl] *n* 道德上的教訓；寓意

you have of putting things!'

'It's a mineral, I *think*,' said Alice.

'Of course it is,' said the Duchess, who seemed ready to agree to everything that Alice said; 'there's a large mustard-mine near here. And the moral of that is—"The more there is of mine, the less there is of yours."'

'Oh, I know!' exclaimed Alice, who had not attended to this last remark, 'it's a vegetable. It doesn't look like one, but it is.'

'I quite agree with you,' said the Duchess; 'and the moral of that is—"Be what you would seem to be"—or if you'd like it put more simply—"Never imagine yourself not to be otherwise than what it might appear to others that what you were or might have been was not otherwise than what you had been would have appeared to them to be otherwise."'

'I think I should understand that better,' Alice said very politely, 'if I had it written down: but I can't quite follow it as you say it.'

'That's nothing to what I could say if I chose,' the Duchess replied, in a pleased tone.

'Pray don't trouble yourself to say it any longer than that,' said Alice.

'Oh, don't talk about trouble!' said the Duchess. 'I make you a present of everything I've said as yet.'

'A cheap sort of present!' thought Alice. 'I'm glad

they don't give birthday presents like that!' But she did not venture to say it out loud.

'Thinking again?' the Duchess asked, with another dig of her sharp little chin.

'I've a right to think,' said Alice sharply, for she was beginning to feel a little worried.

'Just about as much right,' said the Duchess, 'as pigs have to fly; and the m—'

But here, to Alice's great surprise, the Duchess's voice died away, even in the middle of her favourite word 'moral,' and the arm that was linked into hers began to tremble. Alice looked up, and there stood the Queen in front of them, with her arms folded, frowning like a thunderstorm.

'A fine day, your Majesty!' the Duchess began in a low, weak voice.

'Now, I give you fair warning,' shouted the Queen, stamping on the ground as she spoke; 'either you or your head must be off, and that in about half no time! Take your choice!'

The Duchess took her choice, and was gone in a moment.

'Let's go on with the game,' the Queen said to Alice; and Alice was too much frightened to say a word, but slowly followed her back to the croquet-ground.

The other guests had taken advantage of the Queen's

absence, and were resting in the shade: however, the moment they saw her, they hurried back to the game, the Queen merely remarking that a moment's delay would cost them their lives.

All the time they were playing the Queen never left off quarrelling with the other players, and shouting 'Off with his head!' or 'Off with her head!' Those whom she sentenced were taken into custody by the soldiers, who of course had to leave off being arches to do this, so that by the end of half an hour or so there were no arches left, and all the players, except the King, the Queen, and Alice, were in custody and under sentence of execution.

Then the Queen left off, quite out of breath, and said to Alice, 'Have you seen the Mock Turtle yet?'

'No,' said Alice. 'I don't even know what a Mock Turtle is.'

'It's the thing Mock Turtle Soup is made from,' said the Queen.

'I never saw one, or heard of one,' said Alice.

'Come on, then,' said the Queen, 'and he shall tell you his history,'

As they walked off together, Alice heard the King say

custody [ˈkʌstədɪ] *n* 拘留；監禁

in a low voice, to the company generally, 'You are all pardoned.' 'Come, *that's* a good thing!' she said to herself, for she had felt quite unhappy at the number of executions the Queen had ordered.

They very soon came upon a Gryphon, lying fast asleep in the sun. (If you don't know what a Gryphon is, look at the picture.) 'Up, lazy thing!' said the Queen, 'and take this young lady to see the Mock Turtle, and to hear his history. I must go back and see after some executions I have ordered'; and she walked off, leaving Alice alone with the Gryphon. Alice did not quite like the look of the creature, but on the whole she thought it would be quite

as safe to stay with it as to go after that savage Queen: so she waited.

The Gryphon sat up and rubbed its eyes: then it watched the Queen till she was out of sight: then it chuckled. 'What fun!' said the Gryphon, half to itself, half to Alice.

'What *is* the fun?' said Alice.

'Why, *she*,' said the Gryphon. 'It's all her fancy, that: they never executes nobody, you know. Come on!'

'Everybody says "come on!" here,' thought Alice, as she went slowly after it: 'I never was so ordered about in all my life, never!'

They had not gone far before they saw the Mock Turtle in the distance, sitting sad and lonely on a little ledge of rock, and, as they came nearer, Alice could hear him sighing as if his heart would break. She pitied him deeply. 'What is his sorrow?' she asked the Gryphon, and the Gryphon answered, very nearly in the same words as before, 'It's all his fancy, that: he hasn't got no sorrow, you know. Come on!'

So they went up to the Mock Turtle, who looked at them with large eyes full of tears, but said nothing.

'This here young lady,' said the Gryphon, 'she wants for to know your history, she do.'

'I'll tell it her,' said the Mock Turtle in a deep, hollow tone: 'sit down, both of you, and don't speak a word till I've finished.'

So they sat down, and nobody spoke for some minutes. Alice thought to herself, 'I don't see how he can *ever* finish, if he doesn't begin.' But she waited patiently.

'Once,' said the Mock Turtle at last, with a deep sigh, 'I was a real Turtle.'

These words were followed by a very long silence, broken only by an occasional exclamation of 'Hjckrrh!'

from the Gryphon, and the constant heavy sobbing of the Mock Turtle. Alice was very nearly getting up and saying, 'Thank you, sir, for your interesting story,' but she could not help thinking there *must* be more to come, so she sat still and said nothing.

'When we were little,' the Mock Turtle went on at last, more calmly, though still sobbing a little now and then, 'we went to school in the sea. The master was an old Turtle—we used to call him Tortoise—'

'Why did you call him Tortoise, if he wasn't one?' Alice asked.

'We called him Tortoise because he taught us,' said the Mock Turtle angrily: 'really you are very dull!'

'You ought to be ashamed of yourself for asking such a simple question,' added the Gryphon; and then they both sat silent and looked at poor Alice, who felt ready to sink into the earth. At last the Gryphon said to the Mock Turtle, 'Drive on, old fellow! Don't be all day about it!' and he went on in these words:

'Yes, we went to school in the sea, though you mayn't believe it—'

'I never said I didn't!' interrupted Alice.

'You did,' said the Mock Turtle.

'Hold your tongue!' added the Gryphon, before Alice could speak again. The Mock Turtle went on.

'We had the best of educations—in fact, we went to

school every day—'

'*I've* been to a day-school, too,' said Alice; 'you needn't be so proud as all that.'

'With extras?' asked the Mock Turtle a little anxiously.

'Yes,' said Alice, 'we learned French and music.'

'And washing?' said the Mock Turtle.

'Certainly not!' said Alice indignantly.

'Ah! then yours wasn't a really good school,' said the Mock Turtle in a tone of great relief. 'Now at *ours* they had at the end of the bill, "French, music, *and washing—* extra."'

'You couldn't have wanted it much,' said Alice; 'living at the bottom of the sea.'

'I couldn't afford to learn it.' said the Mock Turtle with a sigh. 'I only took the regular course.'

'What was that?' inquired Alice.

'Reeling and Writhing, of course, to begin with,' the Mock Turtle replied; 'and then the different branches of Arithmetic—Ambition, Distraction, Uglification, and Derision.'

'I never heard of "Uglification,"' Alice ventured to say. 'What is it?'

indignantly [ɪnˈdɪgnəntlɪ] *adv* 憤怒地；憤慨地，憤憤不平地

The Gryphon lifted up both its paws in surprise. 'What! Never heard of uglifying!' it exclaimed. 'You know what to beautify is, I suppose?'

'Yes,' said Alice doubtfully: 'it means—to—make—anything—prettier.'

'Well, then,' the Gryphon went on, 'if you don't know what to uglify is, you *are* a simpleton.'

Alice did not feel encouraged to ask any more questions about it, so she turned to the Mock Turtle, and said 'What else had you to learn?'

'Well, there was Mystery,' the Mock Turtle replied, counting off the subjects on his flappers, '—Mystery, ancient and modern, with Seaography: then Drawling—the Drawling-master was an old conger-eel, that used to come once a week: *he* taught us Drawling, Stretching, and Fainting in Coils.'

'What was *that* like?' said Alice.

'Well, I can't show it you myself,' the Mock Turtle said: 'I'm too stiff. And the Gryphon never learnt it.'

'Hadn't time,' said the Gryphon: 'I went to the Classics master, though. He was an old crab, *he* was.'

'I never went to him,' the Mock Turtle said with a sigh: 'he taught Laughing and Grief, they used to say.'

'So he did, so he did,' said the Gryphon, sighing in his turn; and both creatures hid their faces in their paws.

'And how many hours a day did you do lessons?' said

Alice, in a hurry to change the subject.

'Ten hours the first day,' said the Mock Turtle: 'nine the next, and so on.'

'What a curious plan!' exclaimed Alice.

'That's the reason they're called lessons,' the Gryphon remarked: 'because they lessen from day to day.'

This was quite a new idea to Alice, and she thought it over a little before she made her next remark. 'Then the eleventh day must have been a holiday?'

'Of course it was,' said the Mock Turtle.

'And how did you manage on the twelfth?' Alice went on eagerly.

'That's enough about lessons,' the Gryphon interrupted in a very decided tone: 'tell her something about the games now.'

curious [ˈkjʊrɪəs] *adj* 奇怪的；稀奇古怪的，難以理解的

10

The Lobster Quadrille

The Mock Turtle sighed deeply, and drew the back of one flapper across his eyes. He looked at Alice, and tried to speak, but for a minute or two sobs choked his voice. 'Same as if he had a bone in his throat,' said the Gryphon: and it set to work shaking him and punching him in the back. At last the Mock Turtle recovered his voice, and, with tears running down his cheeks, he went on again:—

'You may not have lived much under the sea—' ('I haven't,' said Alice)—'and perhaps you were never even introduced to a lobster—' (Alice began to say 'I once tasted—' but checked herself hastily, and said 'No, never') '—so you can have no idea what a delightful thing a Lobster Quadrille is!'

'No, indeed,' said Alice. 'What sort of a dance is it?'

quadrille [kwəd'rɪl] *n* 四對舞伴的方舞；方舞舞曲

'Why,' said the Gryphon, 'you first form into a line along the sea-shore—'

'Two lines!' cried the Mock Turtle. 'Seals, turtles, salmon, and so on; then, when you've cleared all the jelly-fish out of the way—'

'*That* generally takes some time,' interrupted the Gryphon.

'—you advance twice—'

'Each with a lobster as a partner!' cried the Gryphon.

'Of course,' the Mock Turtle said: 'advance twice, set to partners—'

'—change lobsters, and retire in same order,' continued the Gryphon.

'Then, you know,' the Mock Turtle went on, 'you throw the—'

'The lobsters!' shouted the Gryphon, with a bound into the air.

'—as far out to sea as you can—'

'Swim after them!' screamed the Gryphon.

'Turn a somersault in the sea!' cried the Mock Turtle, capering wildly about.

'Change lobsters again!' yelled the Gryphon at the top

caper ['kepə] *v* 雀躍，蹦跳

of its voice.

'Back to land again, and that's all the first figure,' said the Mock Turtle, suddenly dropping his voice; and the two creatures, who had been jumping about like mad things all this time, sat down again very sadly and quietly, and looked at Alice.

'It must be a very pretty dance,' said Alice timidly.

'Would you like to see a little of it?' said the Mock Turtle.

'Very much indeed,' said Alice.

'Come, let's try the first figure!' said the Mock Turtle to the Gryphon. 'We can do without lobsters, you know. Which shall sing?'

'Oh, *you* sing,' said the Gryphon. 'I've forgotten the words.'

So they began solemnly dancing round and round Alice, every now and then treading on her toes when they passed too close, and waving their forepaws to mark the time, while the Mock Turtle sang this, very slowly and sadly:—

'"Will you walk a little faster?" said a whiting to a snail.
"There's a porpoise close behind us, and he's treading on my tail.

tread [trɛd] **v** 踩，踏；在⋯⋯上面走

See how eagerly the lobsters and the turtles all advance!
They are waiting on the shingle—will you come and join the dance?

Will you, won't you, will you, won't you, will you join the dance?
Will you, won't you, will you, won't you, won't you join the dance?

"You can really have no notion how delightful it will be
When they take us up and throw us, with the lobsters, out to sea!"
But the snail replied "Too far, too far!" and gave a look askance—
Said he thanked the whiting kindly, but he would not join the dance.

Would not, could not, would not, could not, would not join the dance.
Would not, could not, would not, could not, could not join the dance.

'"What matters it how far we go?" his scaly friend replied.
"There is another shore, you know, upon the other side.
The further off from England the nearer is to France—
Then turn not pale, beloved snail, but come and join the dance.

Will you, won't you, will you, won't you, will you join the dance?
Will you, won't you, will you, won't you, won't you join the dance?"'

'Thank you, it's a very interesting dance to watch,' said Alice, feeling very glad that it was over at last: 'and I do so like that curious song about the whiting!'

'Oh, as to the whiting,' said the Mock Turtle, 'they—you've seen them, of course?'

'Yes,' said Alice, 'I've often seen them at dinn—' she checked herself hastily.

askance [əˈskæns] *adj* 懷疑地；不讚許地

'I don't know where Dinn may be,' said the Mock Turtle, 'but if you've seen them so often, of course you know what they're like.'

'I believe so,' Alice replied thoughtfully. 'They have their tails in their mouths—and they're all over crumbs.'

'You're wrong about the crumbs,' said the Mock Turtle: 'crumbs would all wash off in the sea. But they *have* their tails in their mouths; and the reason is—' here the Mock Turtle yawned and shut his eyes.—'Tell her about the reason and all that,' he said to the Gryphon.

'The reason is,' said the Gryphon, 'that they *would* go with the lobsters to the dance. So they got thrown out to sea. So they had to fall a long way. So they got their tails fast in their mouths. So they couldn't get them out again. That's all.'

'Thank you,' said Alice, 'it's very interesting. I never knew so much about a whiting before.'

'I can tell you more than that, if you like,' said the Gryphon. 'Do you know why it's called a whiting?'

'I never thought about it,' said Alice. 'Why?'

'*It does the boots and shoes*,' the Gryphon replied very solemnly.

solemnly [ˈsɑləmlɪ] *adv* 莊嚴地；嚴肅地

Alice was thoroughly puzzled. 'Does the boots and shoes!' she repeated in a wondering tone.

'Why, what are *your* shoes done with?' said the Gryphon. 'I mean, what makes them so shiny?'

Alice looked down at them, and considered a little before she gave her answer. 'They're done with blacking, I believe.'

'Boots and shoes under the sea,' the Gryphon went on in a deep voice, 'are done with a whiting. Now you know.'

'And what are they made of?' Alice asked in a tone of great curiosity.

'Soles and eels, of course,' the Gryphon replied rather impatiently: 'any shrimp could have told you that.'

'If I'd been the whiting,' said Alice, whose thoughts were still running on the song, 'I'd have said to the porpoise, "Keep back, please: we don't want *you* with us!"'

'They were obliged to have him with them,' the Mock Turtle said: 'no wise fish would go anywhere without a porpoise.'

'Wouldn't it really?' said Alice in a tone of great surprise.

'Of course not,' said the Mock Turtle: 'why, if a fish came to *me*, and told me he was going a journey, I should say "With what porpoise?"'

'Don't you mean "purpose"?' said Alice.

'I mean what I say,' the Mock Turtle replied in an offended tone. And the Gryphon added 'Come, let's hear some of *your* adventures.'

'I could tell you my adventures—beginning from this morning,' said Alice a little timidly: 'but it's no use going back to yesterday, because I was a different person then.'

'Explain all that,' said the Mock Turtle.

'No, no! The adventures first,' said the Gryphon in an impatient tone: 'explanations take such a dreadful time.'

So Alice began telling them her adventures from the time when she first saw the White Rabbit. She was a little nervous about it just at first, the two creatures got so close to her, one on each side, and opened their eyes and mouths so *very* wide, but she gained courage as she went on. Her listeners were perfectly quiet till she got to the part about her repeating '*You are old, Father William,*' to the Caterpillar, and the words all coming different, and then the Mock Turtle drew a long breath, and said 'That's very curious.'

'It's all about as curious as it can be,' said the Gryphon.

'It all came different!' the Mock Turtle repeated thoughtfully. 'I should like to hear her try and repeat something now. Tell her to begin.' He looked at the Gryphon as if he thought it had some kind of authority over Alice.

'Stand up and repeat "'*Tis the voice of the sluggard* ,"' said the Gryphon.

'How the creatures order one about, and make one repeat lessons!' thought Alice; 'I might as well be at school at once.' However, she got up, and began to repeat it, but her head was so full of the Lobster Quadrille, that she hardly knew what she was saying, and the words came very queer indeed:—

"Tis the voice of the Lobster; I heard him declare,
"You have baked me too brown, I must sugar my hair."
As a duck with its eyelids, so he with his nose
Trims his belt and his buttons, and turns out his toes.'

[later editions continued as follows
When the sands are all dry, he is gay as a lark,
And will talk in contemptuous tones of the Shark,
But, when the tide rises and sharks are around,
His voice has a timid and tremulous sound.]

'That's different from what *I* used to say when I was a child,' said the Gryphon.

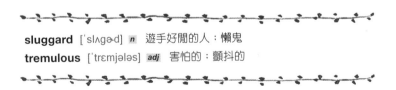

sluggard ['slʌgə-d] *n* 遊手好閒的人；懶鬼
tremulous ['trɛmjələs] *adj* 害怕的；顫抖的

'Well, I never heard it before,' said the Mock Turtle; 'but it sounds uncommon nonsense.'

Alice said nothing; she had sat down with her face in her hands, wondering if anything would *ever* happen in a natural way again.

'I should like to have it explained,' said the Mock Turtle.

'She can't explain it,' said the Gryphon hastily. 'Go on with the next verse.'

'But about his toes?' the Mock Turtle persisted. 'How *could* he turn them out with his nose, you know?'

'It's the first position in dancing.' Alice said; but was dreadfully puzzled by the whole thing, and longed to change the subject.

'Go on with the next verse,' the Gryphon repeated impatiently: 'it begins "*I passed by his garden.*"'

Alice did not dare to disobey, though she felt sure it would all come wrong, and she went on in a trembling voice:—

'I passed by his garden, and marked, with one eye,
How the Owl and the Panther were sharing a pie—'

[later editions continued as follows
The Panther took pie-crust, and gravy, and meat,
While the Owl had the dish as its share of the treat.
When the pie was all finished, the Owl, as a boon,
Was kindly permitted to pocket the spoon:
While the Panther received knife and fork with a growl,
And concluded the banquet—]

'What *is* the use of repeating all that stuff,' the Mock Turtle interrupted, 'if you don't explain it as you go on? It's by far the most confusing thing *I* ever heard!'

'Yes, I think you'd better leave off,' said the Gryphon: and Alice was only too glad to do so.

'Shall we try another figure of the Lobster Quadrille?' the Gryphon went on. 'Or would you like the Mock Turtle to sing you a song?'

'Oh, a song, please, if the Mock Turtle would be so kind,' Alice replied, so eagerly that the Gryphon said, in a rather offended tone, 'Hm! No accounting for tastes! Sing her "*Turtle Soup*," will you, old fellow?'

The Mock Turtle sighed deeply, and began, in a voice sometimes choked with sobs, to sing this:—

'Beautiful Soup, so rich and green,

Waiting in a hot tureen!
Who for such dainties would not stoop?
Soup of the evening, beautiful Soup!
Soup of the evening, beautiful Soup!
Beau—ootiful Soo—oop!
Beau—ootiful Soo—oop!
Soo—oop of the e—e—evening,
Beautiful, beautiful Soup!

'Beautiful Soup! Who cares for fish,
Game, or any other dish?
Who would not give all else for two
Pennyworth only of beautiful Soup?
Pennyworth only of beautiful Soup?
Beau—ootiful Soo—oop!
Beau—ootiful Soo—oop!
Soo—oop of the e—e—evening,
Beautiful, beauti—FUL SOUP!'

'Chorus again!' cried the Gryphon, and the Mock Turtle had just begun to repeat it, when a cry of 'The trial's beginning!' was heard in the distance.

'Come on!' cried the Gryphon, and, taking Alice by

tureen [tjʊˈrin] *n* 砂鍋：焙盤

the hand, it hurried off, without waiting for the end of the song.

'What trial is it?' Alice panted as she ran; but the Gryphon only answered 'Come on!' and ran the faster, while more and more faintly came, carried on the breeze that followed them, the melancholy words:—

'Soo—oop of the e—e—evening,
Beautiful, beautiful Soup!'

11 /

Who Stole the Tarts?

The King and Queen of Hearts were seated on their throne when they arrived, with a great crowd assembled about them—all sorts of little birds and beasts, as well as the whole pack of cards: the Knave was standing before them, in chains, with a soldier on each side to guard him; and near the King was the White Rabbit, with a trumpet in one hand, and a scroll of

scroll [skrol] *n* 卷軸；名冊

parchment in the other. In the very middle of the court was a table, with a large dish of tarts upon it: they looked so good, that it made Alice quite hungry to look at them—'I wish they'd get the trial done,' she thought, 'and hand round the refreshments!' But there seemed to be no chance of this, so she began looking at everything about her, to pass away the time.

Alice had never been in a court of justice before, but she had read about them in books, and she was quite pleased to find that she knew the name of nearly everything there. 'That's the judge,' she said to herself, 'because of his great wig.'

The judge, by the way, was the King; and as he wore his crown over the wig, (look at the frontispiece if you want to see how he did it,) he did not look at all comfortable, and it was certainly not becoming.

'And that's the jury-box,' thought Alice, 'and those twelve creatures,' (she was obliged to say 'creatures,' you see, because some of them were animals, and some were birds,) 'I suppose they are the jurors.' She said this last word two or three times over to herself, being rather

parchment [ˈpɑrtʃmənt] *n* 羊皮紙
becoming [bɪˈkʌmɪŋ] *adj* 合適的，適宜的

proud of it: for she thought, and rightly too, that very few little girls of her age knew the meaning of it at all. However, 'jury-men' would have done just as well.

The twelve jurors were all writing very busily on slates. 'What are they doing?' Alice whispered to the Gryphon. 'They can't have anything to put down yet, before the trial's begun.'

'They're putting down their names,' the Gryphon whispered in reply, 'for fear they should forget them before the end of the trial.'

'Stupid things!' Alice began in a loud, indignant voice, but she stopped hastily, for the White Rabbit cried out, 'Silence in the court!' and the King put on his spectacles and looked anxiously round, to make out who was talking.

Alice could see, as well as if she were looking over their shoulders, that all the jurors were writing down 'stupid things!' on their slates, and she could even make out that one of them didn't know how to spell 'stupid,' and that he had to ask his neighbour to tell him. 'A nice muddle their slates'll be in before the trial's over!' thought Alice.

One of the jurors had a pencil that squeaked. This of

spectacle [ˈspɛktəkl̩] *n* 眼鏡
muddle [ˈmʌdl̩] *n* 糊塗；混亂狀態

course, Alice could *not* stand, and she went round the court and got behind him, and very soon found an opportunity of taking it away. She did it so quickly that the poor little juror (it was Bill, the Lizard) could not make out at all what had become of it; so, after hunting all about for it, he was obliged to write with one finger for the rest of the day; and this was of very little use, as it left no mark on the slate.

'Herald, read the accusation!' said the King.

On this the White Rabbit blew three blasts on the trumpet, and then unrolled the parchment scroll, and read as follows:—

'The Queen of Hearts, she made some tarts,
All on a summer day:
The Knave of Hearts, he stole those tarts,
And took them quite away!'

'Consider your verdict,' the King said to the jury.

'Not yet, not yet!' the Rabbit hastily interrupted. 'There's a great deal to come before that!'

'Call the first witness,' said the King; and the White

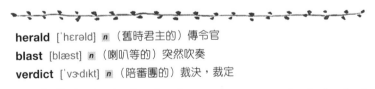

herald [ˈhɛrəld] *n* （舊時君主的）傳令官
blast [blæst] *n* （喇叭等的）突然吹奏
verdict [ˈvɝdɪkt] *n* （陪審團的）裁決，裁定

Rabbit blew three blasts on the trumpet, and called out, 'First witness!'

The first witness was the Hatter. He came in with a teacup in one hand and a piece of bread-and-butter in the other. 'I beg pardon, your Majesty,' he began, 'for bringing these in: but I hadn't quite finished my tea when I was sent for.'

'You ought to have finished,' said the King. 'When did you begin?'

The Hatter looked at the March Hare, who had followed him into the court, arm-in-arm with the Dormouse. 'Fourteenth of March, I *think* it was,' he said.

'Fifteenth,' said the March Hare.

'Sixteenth,' added the Dormouse.

'Write that down,' the King said to the jury, and the jury eagerly wrote down all three dates on their slates, and then added them up, and reduced the answer to shillings and pence.

'Take off your hat,' the King said to the Hatter.

'It isn't mine,' said the Hatter.

'*Stolen*!' the King exclaimed, turning to the jury, who instantly made a memorandum of the fact.

'I keep them to sell,' the Hatter added as an explanation; 'I've none of my own. I'm a hatter.'

Here the Queen put on her spectacles, and began staring at the Hatter, who turned pale and fidgeted.

'Give your evidence,' said the King; 'and don't be nervous, or I'll have you executed on the spot.'

This did not seem to encourage the witness at all: he kept shifting from one foot to the other, looking uneasily at the Queen, and in his confusion he bit a large piece out of his teacup instead of the bread-and-butter.

Just at this moment Alice felt a very curious sensation, which puzzled her a good deal until she made out what it was: she was beginning to grow larger again, and she thought at first she would get up and leave the court; but on second thoughts she decided to remain where she was as long as there was room for her.

'I wish you wouldn't squeeze so.' said the Dormouse, who was sitting next to her. 'I can hardly breathe.'

'I can't help it,' said Alice very meekly: 'I'm growing.'

'You've no right to grow *here*,' said the Dormouse.

fidgeted ['fɪdʒɪtɪd] *adj* 煩躁的，坐立不安的

'Don't talk nonsense,' said Alice more boldly: 'you know you're growing too.'

'Yes, but *I* grow at a reasonable pace,' said the Dormouse: 'not in that ridiculous fashion.' And he got up very sulkily and crossed over to the other side of the court.

All this time the Queen had never left off staring at the Hatter, and, just as the Dormouse crossed the court, she said to one of the officers of the court, 'Bring me the list of the singers in the last concert!' on which the wretched Hatter trembled so, that he shook both his shoes off.

'Give your evidence,' the King repeated angrily, 'or I'll have you executed, whether you're nervous or not.'

'I'm a poor man, your Majesty,' the Hatter began, in a trembling voice, '—and I hadn't begun my tea—not above a week or so—and what with the bread-and-butter getting so thin—and the twinkling of the tea—'

'The twinkling of the *what*?' said the King.

'It *began* with the tea,' the Hatter replied.

'Of course twinkling begins with a T!' said the King sharply. 'Do you take me for a dunce? Go on!'

'I'm a poor man,' the Hatter went on, 'and most

dunce [dʌns] *n* 笨蛋，傻瓜

things twinkled after that—only the March Hare said—'

'I didn't!' the March Hare interrupted in a great hurry.

'You did!' said the Hatter.

'I deny it!' said the March Hare.

'He denies it,' said the King: 'leave out that part.'

'Well, at any rate, the Dormouse said—' the Hatter went on, looking anxiously round to see if he would deny it too: but the Dormouse denied nothing, being fast asleep.

'After that,' continued the Hatter, 'I cut some more bread-and-butter—'

'But what did the Dormouse say?' one of the jury asked.

'That I can't remember,' said the Hatter.

'You *must* remember,' remarked the King, 'or I'll have you executed.'

The miserable Hatter dropped his teacup and bread-and-butter, and went down on one knee. 'I'm a poor man, your Majesty,' he began.

'You're a *very* poor *speaker*,' said the King.

Here one of the guinea-pigs cheered, and was immediately suppressed by the officers of the court. (As

suppress [sə'prɛs] *v* 制止：壓制

that is rather a hard word, I will just explain to you how it was done. They had a large canvas bag, which tied up at the mouth with strings: into this they slipped the guinea-pig, head first, and then sat upon it.)

'I'm glad I've seen that done,' thought Alice. 'I've so often read in the newspapers, at the end of trials, "There was some attempts at applause, which was immediately suppressed by the officers of the court," and I never understood what it meant till now.'

'If that's all you know about it, you may stand down,' continued the King.

'I can't go no lower,' said the Hatter: 'I'm on the floor, as it is.'

'Then you may *sit* down,' the King replied.

Here the other guinea-pig cheered, and was suppressed.

'Come, that finished the guinea-pigs!' thought Alice. 'Now we shall get on better.'

'I'd rather finish my tea,' said the Hatter, with an anxious look at the Queen, who was reading the list of singers.

'You may go,' said the King, and the Hatter hurriedly left the court, without even waiting to put his shoes on.

'—and just take his head off outside,' the Queen added to one of the officers: but the Hatter was out of sight before the officer could get to the door.

'Call the next witness!' said the King.

The next witness was the Duchess's cook. She carried the pepper-box in her hand, and Alice guessed who it was, even before she got into the court, by the way the people near the door began sneezing all at once.

'Give your evidence,' said the King.

'Shan't,' said the cook.

The King looked anxiously at the White Rabbit, who said in a low voice, 'Your Majesty must cross-examine *this* witness.'

'Well, if I must, I must,' the King said, with a melancholy air, and, after folding his arms and frowning at the cook till his eyes were nearly out of sight, he said in a deep voice, 'What are tarts made of?'

'Pepper, mostly,' said the cook.

'Treacle,' said a sleepy voice behind her.

'Collar that Dormouse,' the Queen shrieked out. 'Behead that Dormouse! Turn that Dormouse out of court! Suppress him! Pinch him! Off with his whiskers!'

For some minutes the whole court was in confusion, getting the Dormouse turned out, and, by the time they had settled down again, the cook had disappeared.

'Never mind!' said the King, with an air of great relief. 'Call the next witness.' And he added in an undertone to the Queen, 'Really, my dear, *you* must cross-examine the next witness. It quite makes my forehead ache!'

Alice watched the White Rabbit as he fumbled over the list, feeling very curious to see what the next witness would be like, '—for they haven't got much evidence *yet*,' she said to herself. Imagine her surprise, when the White Rabbit read out, at the top of his shrill little voice, the name 'Alice!'

12

Alice's Evidence

'Here!' cried Alice, quite forgetting in the flurry of the moment how large she had grown in the last few minutes, and she jumped up in such a hurry that she

tipped over the jury-box with the edge of her skirt, upsetting all the jurymen on to the heads of the crowd below, and there they lay sprawling about, reminding her very much of a globe of goldfish she had accidentally upset the week before.

'Oh, I *beg* your pardon!' she exclaimed in a tone of great dismay, and began picking them up again as quickly as she could, for the accident of the goldfish kept running in her head, and she had a vague sort of idea that they must be collected at once and put back into the jury-box, or they would die.

'The trial cannot proceed,' said the King in a very grave voice, 'until all the jurymen are back in their proper places—*all*,' he repeated with great emphasis, looking hard at Alice as he said do.

Alice looked at the jury-box, and saw that, in her haste, she had put the Lizard in head downwards, and the poor little thing was waving its tail about in a melancholy way, being quite unable to move. She soon got it out again, and put it right; 'not that it signifies much,' she said to herself; 'I should think it would be *quite* as much use in

dismay [dɪsˈme] *n* 驚慌，沮喪，氣餒
vague [veg] *adj* 不明確的；曖昧的，含糊的

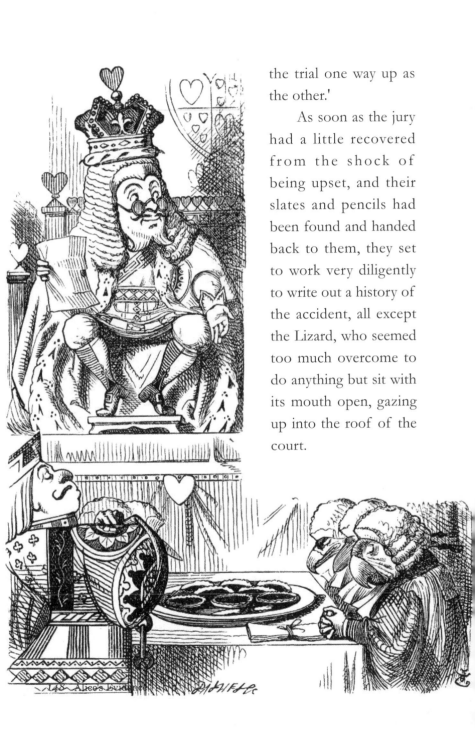

the trial one way up as the other.'

As soon as the jury had a little recovered from the shock of being upset, and their slates and pencils had been found and handed back to them, they set to work very diligently to write out a history of the accident, all except the Lizard, who seemed too much overcome to do anything but sit with its mouth open, gazing up into the roof of the court.

'What do you know about this business?' the King said to Alice.

'Nothing,' said Alice.

'Nothing *whatever*?' persisted the King.

'Nothing whatever,' said Alice.

'That's very important,' the King said, turning to the jury. They were just beginning to write this down on their slates, when the White Rabbit interrupted: '*Uni*mportant, your Majesty means, of course,' he said in a very respectful tone, but frowning and making faces at him as he spoke.

'*Uni*mportant, of course, I meant,' the King hastily said, and went on to himself in an undertone, 'important—unimportant—unimportant— important—' as if he were trying which word sounded best.

Some of the jury wrote it down 'important,' and some 'unimportant.' Alice could see this, as she was near enough to look over their slates; 'but it doesn't matter a bit,' she thought to herself.

At this moment the King, who had been for some time busily writing in his note-book, cackled out 'Silence!' and read out from his book, 'Rule Forty-two. *All persons more than a mile high to leave the court.*'

Everybody looked at Alice.

'*I'm* not a mile high,' said Alice.

'You are,' said the King.

'Nearly two miles high,' added the Queen.

'Well, I shan't go, at any rate,' said Alice: 'besides, that's not a regular rule: you invented it just now.'

'It's the oldest rule in the book,' said the King.

'Then it ought to be Number One,' said Alice.

The King turned pale, and shut his note-book hastily. 'Consider your verdict,' he said to the jury, in a low, trembling voice.

'There's more evidence to come yet, please your Majesty,' said the White Rabbit, jumping up in a great hurry; 'this paper has just been picked up.'

'What's in it?' said the Queen.

'I haven't opened it yet,' said the White Rabbit, 'but it seems to be a letter, written by the prisoner to—to somebody.'

'It must have been that,' said the King, 'unless it was written to nobody, which isn't usual, you know.'

'Who is it directed to?' said one of the jurymen.

'It isn't directed at all,' said the White Rabbit; 'in fact, there's nothing written on the *outside*.' He unfolded the paper as he spoke, and added 'It isn't a letter, after all: it's a set of verses.'

'Are they in the prisoner's handwriting?' asked another of the jurymen.

'No, they're not,' said the White Rabbit, 'and that's the queerest thing about it.' (The jury all looked puzzled.)

'He must have imitated somebody else's hand,' said

the King. (The jury all brightened up again.)

'Please your Majesty,' said the Knave, 'I didn't write it, and they can't prove I did: there's no name signed at the end.'

'If you didn't sign it,' said the King, 'that only makes the matter worse. You *must* have meant some mischief, or else you'd have signed your name like an honest man.'

There was a general clapping of hands at this: it was the first really clever thing the King had said that day.

'That *proves* his guilt,' said the Queen.

'It proves nothing of the sort!' said Alice. 'Why, you don't even know what they're about!'

'Read them,' said the King.

The White Rabbit put on his spectacles. 'Where shall I begin, please your Majesty?' he asked.

'Begin at the beginning,' the King said gravely, 'and go on till you come to the end: then stop.'

These were the verses the White Rabbit read:—

'They told me you had been to her,
And mentioned me to him:
She gave me a good character,
But said I could not swim.

mischief [ˈmɪstʃɪf] *n* 狡猾，不實；胡鬧，惡作劇

He sent them word I had not gone
(We know it to be true):
If she should push the matter on,
What would become of you?

I gave her one, they gave him two,
You gave us three or more;
They all returned from him to you,
Though they were mine before.

If I or she should chance to be
Involved in this affair,
He trusts to you to set them free,
Exactly as we were.

My notion was that you had been
(Before she had this fit)
An obstacle that came between
Him, and ourselves, and it.

Don't let him know she liked them best,
For this must ever be

obstacle [ˈɑbstəkl] *n* 障礙（物）；妨礙

A secret, kept from all the rest,
Between yourself and me.'

'That's the most important piece of evidence we've heard yet,' said the King, rubbing his hands; 'so now let the jury—'

'If any one of them can explain it,' said Alice, (she had grown so large in the last few minutes that she wasn't a bit afraid of interrupting him,) 'I'll give him sixpence. *I* don't believe there's an atom of meaning in it.'

The jury all wrote down on their slates, '*She* doesn't believe there's an atom of meaning in it,' but none of them attempted to explain the paper.

'If there's no meaning in it,' said the King, 'that saves a world of trouble, you know, as we needn't try to find any. And yet I don't know,' he went on, spreading out the verses on his knee, and looking at them with one eye; 'I seem to see some meaning in them, after all. "*—said I could not swim—*" you can't swim, can you?' he added, turning to the Knave.

The Knave shook his head sadly. 'Do I look like it?' he said. (Which he certainly did *not*, being made entirely of cardboard.)

'All right, so far,' said the King, and he went on muttering over the verses to himself: '"*We know it to be true—*" that's the jury, of course—"*I gave her one, they gave him two—*" why, that must be what he did with the

tarts, you know—'

'But, it goes on "*they all returned from him to you,*"' said Alice.

'Why, there they are!' said the King triumphantly, pointing to the tarts on the table. 'Nothing can be clearer than *that*. Then again—"*before she had this fit*—" you never had fits, my dear, I think?' he said to the Queen.

'Never!' said the Queen furiously, throwing an inkstand at the Lizard as she spoke. (The unfortunate little Bill had left off writing on his slate with one finger, as he found it made no mark; but he now hastily began again, using the ink, that was trickling down his face, as long as it lasted.)

'Then the words don't *fit* you,' said the King, looking round the court with a smile. There was a dead silence.

'It's a pun!' the King added in an offended tone, and everybody laughed, 'Let the jury consider their verdict,' the King said, for about the twentieth time that day.

'No, no!' said the Queen. 'Sentence first—verdict afterwards.'

'Stuff and nonsense!' said Alice loudly. 'The idea of having the sentence first!'

'Hold your tongue!' said the Queen, turning purple.

pun [pʌn] *n* 雙關語

'I won't!' said Alice.

'Off with her head!' the Queen shouted at the top of her voice. Nobody moved.

'Who cares for you?' said Alice, (she had grown to her full size by this time.) 'You're nothing but a pack of cards!'

At this the whole pack rose up into the air, and came flying down upon her: she gave a little scream, half of fright and half of anger, and tried to beat them off, and found herself lying on the bank, with her head in the lap of her sister, who was gently brushing away some dead leaves that had fluttered down from the trees upon her face.

'Wake up, Alice dear!' said her sister; 'Why, what a long sleep you've had!'

'Oh, I've had such a curious dream!' said Alice, and she told her sister, as well as she could remember them, all these strange Adventures of hers that you have just been reading about; and when she had finished, her sister kissed her, and said, 'It *was* a curious dream, dear, certainly: but now run in to your tea; it's getting late.' So Alice got up and ran off, thinking while she ran, as well she might, what a wonderful dream it had been.

But her sister sat still just as she left her, leaning her head on her hand, watching the setting sun, and thinking of little Alice and all her wonderful Adventures, till she too began dreaming after a fashion, and this was her dream:—

First, she dreamed of little Alice herself, and once again the tiny hands were clasped upon her knee, and the bright eager eyes were looking up into hers—she could hear the very tones of her voice, and see that queer little toss of her head to keep back the wandering hair that

would always get into her eyes—and still as she listened, or seemed to listen, the whole place around her became alive with the strange creatures of her little sister's dream.

The long grass rustled at her feet as the White Rabbit hurried by—the frightened Mouse splashed his way through the neighbouring pool—she could hear the rattle of the teacups as the March Hare and his friends shared their never-ending meal, and the shrill voice of the Queen ordering off her unfortunate guests to execution—once more the pig-baby was sneezing on the Duchess's knee, while plates and dishes crashed around it—once more the shriek of the Gryphon, the squeaking of the Lizard's slate-pencil, and the choking of the suppressed guinea-pigs, filled the air, mixed up with the distant sobs of the miserable Mock Turtle.

So she sat on, with closed eyes, and half believed herself in Wonderland, though she knew she had but to open them again, and all would change to dull reality—the grass would be only rustling in the wind, and the pool rippling to the waving of the reeds—the rattling teacups would change to tinkling sheep-bells, and the Queen's shrill cries to the voice of the shepherd boy—and the

shepherd [ˈʃɛpəd] *n* 牧羊人

sneeze of the baby, the shriek of the Gryphon, and all the other queer noises, would change (she knew) to the confused clamour of the busy farm-yard—while the lowing of the cattle in the distance would take the place of the Mock Turtle's heavy sobs.

Lastly, she pictured to herself how this same little sister of hers would, in the after-time, be herself a grown woman; and how she would keep, through all her riper years, the simple and loving heart of her childhood: and how she would gather about her other little children, and make *their* eyes bright and eager with many a strange tale, perhaps even with the dream of Wonderland of long ago: and how she would feel with all their simple sorrows, and find a pleasure in all their simple joys, remembering her own child-life, and the happy summer days.

clamour ['klæmə-] *n* 喧鬧聲
lowing ['loɪŋ] *n* 牛鳴聲
eager ['igə-] *adj* 熱切的；渴望的